CONTENT

ITALIAN SONATA

Italian Sonata is the second volume in the 'Dangerous Desire' series.
The first is *The Gentlemen's Club*, (also released as 'Forbidden Desire')
which may be found on Amazon.

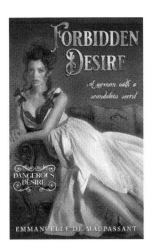

Cover Design by Victoria Cooper

First published in 2017, as 'Italian Sonata' - within the 'Noire' trilogy - and
subsequently published as 'Forbidden Temptation'.

www.emmanuelledemaupassant.com

ITALIAN SONATA

VOLUME TWO IN THE DANGEROUS DESIRE TRILOGY

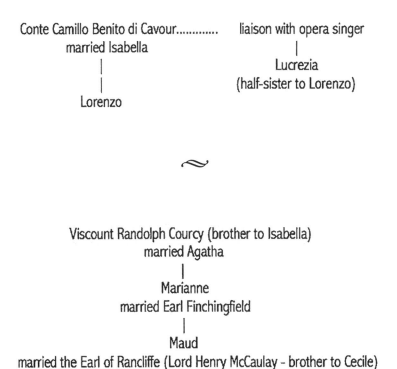

Conte Camillo Benito di Cavour............. liaison with opera singer
married Isabella |
            | Lucrezia
            | (half-sister to Lorenzo)
        Lorenzo

Viscount Randolph Courcy (brother to Isabella)
                married Agatha
                      |
                  Marianne
            married Earl Finchingfield
                      |
                    Maud
married the Earl of Rancliffe (Lord Henry McCaulay - brother to Cecile)

PROLOGUE

NOT FAR FROM SORRENTO, in Southern Italy, where the coast meets the sea in precipitous cliffs, lies Castello di Scogliera, that ancient seat of disdainful nobility. Built upon an island of eternal, wave-lashed rock, the castle is reached by a cobbled causeway—but only at certain times of the day and night, according to the ebb and flow of the tide.

Look up at its narrow windows, and you might imagine yourself watched. Perhaps all old buildings watch. How else might they while away the centuries but in observing their residents. They listen, and remember: secrets and deceptions, memories of joy, and pain.

By night, some of those windows wink, lit by candles or chandeliers. Others stand dark, yet with a knowing glint, reflecting the moon's light from their panes.

Take these stone steps, worn smooth from the tread of generations of di Cavours, and all who serve them. Listen to the rise and fall of the sea, the creaking castle bones, and the cold murmur of granite. Place your hand upon those walls, salt-misted damp, where others have touched.

Tragedy has shaped the inhabitants of the castle in ways we can only imagine.

Come now, and enter, for a fire is blazing in the ancient hearth, and dinner has been set. The wine is poured, and a tale is ready to unfold.

The past does not lie quietly.

1

Late March, 1899

ON A CERTAIN THURSDAY between the hours of ten and eleven, a small party assembled at the church of the Holy Trinity, in the parish of Kensington, just west of Hyde Park Corner, on the Brompton Road.

As the newspapers report, the bride wore a costume more suited to a fancy dress event than a wedding, in the style of an Indian Mughal. Despite the unconventionality of her choice, those in attendance agreed that it suited her well. Her crimson jacket was embroidered with humming birds and bumble bees, accentuated above the hip by a wide, golden sash. From its waistband, she later produced a miniature scimitar, surprising those at the Wedding Breakfast with her dexterity in using it to cut the cake. Emerald drop earrings, a gift from the groom to his bride, peeked from beneath titian curls, artfully tucked into a scarlet turban.

The groom's sister, Lady Cecile, standing as maid-of-honour, was attired more traditionally, in a green velvet suit, puff-sleeved in the Gigot fashion, tapering to a narrow fore-arm, worn with a jaunty hat atop her blonde hair.

Both carried a bouquet of orange blossom and white roses.

Standing before the Almighty, the groom bestowed upon the forehead of his bride a kiss.

It wasn't too late for them to turn back: to take to their heels. Neither were tempted, however. They were exactly where they wished to be. If Rancliffe felt a lurch of uncertainty at the sight of his future wife fluttering her eyes at the handsome young minister waiting for them at the altar, he set this aside. He was a man besotted, and such extremes of love cause us to make light of those foibles from which, under other circumstances, we might flee.

The Earl of Rancliffe had pursued Lady Finchingfield with sufficient steadfastness and ardour, it appeared, for her to allow herself to be caught—although those guests closest to the bride might have speculated as to the terms under which the contract had been made.

Marriage was a covenant to which Maud had pledged never to succumb, in pursuit of feminine liberation and independence. Yet, here she was, allowing her hand to be held and a ring placed upon it. Their vows were spoken in earnestness, and they had promised to be true to one another's desires.

Every inch the blushing bride, her face was flushed with pleasure. How wonderful it is, after all, to find ourselves surprised by the serendipity of our choices.

Only the most cynical would speculate on the significance of Maud's wedded state bringing her access to a handsome sum, placed in trust at her parents' death and released upon her marriage.

As the bride's slippered feet tripped daintily up the aisle, she was thinking already of the warmth of her husband's arms. Perhaps all brides think such things, however pure and simple and modest they appear.

They emerged into spits of sleet. A gust caused Maud to clutch at her groom and so taken was he by the surge of joy in his heart, that he lifted her ostentatiously into his arms, carrying her down the last of the church steps, into the waiting carriage.

'What a devoted couple they make!' exclaimed the priest. 'A true love match, I've no doubt.'

A number of the bride's friends, cheering the newlyweds as they emerged onto the Brompton Road, would have been unknown to readers of *The Times* or *The Illustrated London News*. One might say that their choice of attire was more risqué than was usual for a Society wedding, and the rouge upon their cheeks a little too enthusiastically applied. Among them was the celebrated milliner Ms Tarbuck, who had supplied the headdresses of the bride and her maid-of-honour for this happy occasion.

The bride's great-aunt, Isabella, remembering her bag of confetti, fluttered a handful of rose-petals after the laughing couple.

Eyes bright with happiness, Cecile blew kisses at her brother and his new wife; their joy was her own.

Beside her, shaking the wet from her skirts with a grimace of displeasure, was her Oxfordshire aunt. It wouldn't be long, she supposed, before a match was made for Cecile. She made a mental note to speak severely to Rancliffe on the matter. If other suitors proved wanting, wedlock to her village parson, newly widowed, might prove suitable. He was old enough, and dull enough, to provide a steady, guiding hand.

Yes, thought the Oxfordshire aunt, it's the least I can do.

2

CECILE'S final letter of appraisal, sent from the Beaulieu Academy for Ladies, had stated that her genteel deportment was just as was hoped for 'in a dignified young lady of fashion'. There were other, minor, accomplishments: an elegant writing hand, an ability to recite the great poets, and talent with an embroidery needle, alongside her singing voice and her playing of the pianoforte.

Rancliffe couldn't help but muse on the contrast between Cecile and Maud, who'd attended the very same establishment. Maud's broad knowledge of certain aspects of the natural sciences, and the sharp application of her brain to her own entomological studies, were sufficient to put most men to shame.

However, his sweet Cecile was a model of demureness, patience, and generosity of spirit, readier to think well of others than badly.

She'll make some chap very happy indeed, Rancliffe had often told himself. The necessity of marriage for his sister had long been playing upon his mind, and Maud was inclined to agree.

It would hardly do for Cecile to live always with them, after all.

'Of course, she can hardly be expected to 'discover' a husband for herself,' remarked Maud. 'We must, when the time comes, introduce her to those we think suitable.'

Rancliffe nodded in approval, reminding himself, once again, how fortunate he was in having chosen Maud for his wife. She possessed not only beauty and charm, but wit and brains.

'With the new century knocking at the door, times are changing,' chided the new Countess Rancliffe. 'While a man of notable social standing may not yet expect, or desire, his wife to express *too* strong an opinion on matters of the world, he yet requires her to be the engaging hostess at his table. Some awareness and intellectual comprehension must be cultivated. She has been too much in narrow company. A tour of the European capitals shall be just the thing, and our little Cecile will return far wiser.'

It was true that no man of position wished to be known for having a wife with the mind of a child: no matter that such a quality was prized in his grandfather's time. 'In all things, you're right, my love,' Rancliffe conceded. 'I've been remiss in failing to earlier expose her to the elegance of European culture.'

Without delay, the earl booked their passage across the Channel.

CECILE WAS DELIGHTED. How she'd longed to see the mountains of Switzerland and the medieval towns of the Rhineland, as described in her favourite novels. Packing her trunk, she found room for Mr Wilkie Collins' tales and those of Mrs Braddon, as well as her volumes of *The Mysteries of*

Udolpho, and *The Castle of Otrano*, passed down on her moth-er's side.

English rain spattered the window as they boarded the train from London's Charing Cross, to take them to the coast. But, in her imagination, Cecile was already warmed by the golden, Mediterranean sun.

What will Europe be like? A place of ancient castles, gardens filled with lush blooms and exotic perfumes, and dark-haired, romantic-eyed gentlemen. I might drop my glove and one, bowing, shall return it, meeting my eye for a brief moment. In that mingled glance, our souls will speak.

Her pulse leapt at the thought.

He'll press his hand to his heart and promise eternal adoration. Perhaps...

THE SEA CROSSING wasn't long in duration, which was just as well, since Cecile's stomach was inclined to pitch and heave in sympathy with the boat. How tiresome, just as she was begin-ning her travels! None of the heroines she so admired would suffer from such a weakness, she felt sure.

By the time they boarded the train from Calais to Paris, Cecile had recovered her appetite, and was keen to partake of afternoon tea. However, announcing themselves indisposed, the newlyweds locked themselves into their compartment. From the ensuing moans, Cecile guessed that the motion of the train was afflicting them.

Luckily, her own constitution being restored, Cecile was emboldened to search out the dining car. Not wishing to sit alone, she placed herself at the table of two elderly ladies, who made her most welcome. A pot of Darjeeling and a selection of eclairs and fondant fancies were soon placed before them, and the time passed pleasantly. Old ladies, Cecile found, were always eager to recount tales of their youth, and to share gossip on notable figures of their own sex. The Browne-Huntley sisters were no exception.

'My dear, do look!' declared the first Ms Browne-Huntley, indicating a rising figure at the far end of the car: a woman in a travelling costume of stiff brown cotton, her jacket and skirt bearing an extraordinary number of pockets.

'It's the intrepid Flora McTavish,' said the second, tapping Cecile's hand excitedly.

'Is it?' Cecile craned her neck. 'I've read about her in *The Lady*. I thought she was traversing the Wadi deserts of Jordan and Syria, dressed as a man and riding a camel.'

'She was indeed,' replied the first, 'But she's lately been in London, delivering a series of lectures on the Bedouin tribes. No doubt, she's now setting forth again, to new adventures.'

'How marvellous,' said Cecile, though she couldn't help being shocked at the sun's effect on Ms McTavish's skin; it was far darker than was seemly for a lady.

I must be careful to always wear my hat but, if I truly were an adventuress, travelling to remote jungle villages in the Congo, or to obscure places of spiritual mysticism, in the mountains of Tibet, perhaps I wouldn't care if my nose came to be covered in freckles. I might, even, not mind wearing such drab colours. One must be practical I suppose, when travelling by mule and rickshaw.

'Ah!' announced one of the old ladies, 'We're approaching the outskirts. Time to ready ourselves.'

Cecile made her way down the dining car, still musing on where she might like to travel, were she to follow in Ms McTavish's footsteps, and how large one's baggage might conceivably be under such circumstances.

Entering the corridor to their compartments, she looked out at the Paris skyline. How glorious it was, at last, to be in the city of which she'd read so much, filled with chic Parisiennes, and their handsome beaux.

Meanwhile, another passenger was approaching from the opposing end, his nose pressed not to the view beyond the window but to a map. As they drew level, the train lurched and Cecile found herself thrown against one solid, unyielding chest. Stumbling, she trod heavily on his toes, then lost her balance altogether.

Two great hands were suddenly beneath her arms, lifting her through the air to place her upright. 'Pardon my clumsiness, Ma'am. Let me help you up.'

To her surprise, the voice that spoke was American, and though Cecile had been brought up to consider her cousins from across the Atlantic to be vulgar and noisy, this voice was caramel-buttered, the vowels drawn out like the promise of summer—unlike any voice she'd heard before.

'You're not injured, I hope.' Looking up, she found that the owner of the voice was also unlike any she'd met before: so tall that his hair, golden and curling abundantly from the crown of his head, brushed the ceiling, and so broad that his shoulders filled the width of the passageway.

'The name's Lance Robinson. Pleased to meet you.' He extended his hand. 'Short for Lancelot. My mother's choice. She loved those tales of King Arthur and all those gallant knights of the Round Table, off doing good deeds. S'pose she hoped I'd turn out just the same.'

'And have you?' she asked. 'I mean... I'm sure she's very proud of you.'

'She is that.' The American grinned and Cecile was astonished at the whiteness of his teeth. 'My Pa, too. He's looking to expand into South America, to link the wide-open plains of Argentina with their capital, via railroad. It's my duty to help him in that plan, and my honest pleasure too. I'll be taking the SS *Leviathan* to Rio in three months' time, and then onwards, to Buenos Aires.'

'What a grand adventure that sounds, Mr Robinson.'

If I were to marry, thought Cecile. *You're the sort of man I might like to be married to.*

'I'm headed down through Europe, travellin' the railroads, meetin' various bigwigs, and learnin' all I can.'

'No galleries or museums? Not like a traditional 'Grand Tour'?'

He shook his head and gave a smile that sent Cecile's pulse into a most perturbing rhythm. 'It's all work for me, but I'm havin' a mighty-fine time anyways.'

Cecile looked at his lips as he spoke, and wondered how they might feel pressed against her own. She couldn't help but notice, he was looking right back at her.

They stood, just like that, until the door of her brother's compartment opened, and Cecile heard Henry's voice, calling to her.

'Well, it's been delightful to meet you, Mr Robinson.' Offering him her gloved hand, it was upon the tip of her tongue to ask where he might be staying in Paris, but such forwardness was beyond her. No lady would ask such a thing.

He gave her hand another solid shake. 'Ma'am, the pleasure was all mine.'

PARIS!

The same sooty rain that committed London to sit in mud and dripping grime, bestowed this city with glistening streets, infinitely reflecting the dazzle of its evening illuminations. Perhaps, it had the same perils and filth and overflowing sewers. And yet, our merry party saw only its glittering entertainments, and daring triumphs.

Determined that his bride should enjoy every comfort, Henry had booked the Suite Impériale, at the newly opened Hôtel Ritz, in the 1st arrondissement. Conveniently, there was a modestly-sized adjoining room for Cecile. It was a home from home indeed, with endless hot water in the bathroom. From the ceiling of its grand salon, upholstered in red and gold, hung large chandeliers, their light reflected in the Baroque mirror between the windows, which looked down upon the Place Vendôme.

Retiring for the night, Maud drew the coverlet up to her chin (sumptuous as the room was, the windows did rather let in a draught). 'This bed is said to be identical to that used by Marie Antoinette, in the Palace of Versailles.'

'And we all know how Marie Antoinette kept herself warm,' murmured Henry, his hand moving to the small of his wife's back. As their hips met, his mouth closed upon hers. His chin was bristling from a day's growth: rough on her cheek, rough on her collarbone, rough across her nipple. He descended beneath the covers and, with a contented sigh, Maud took that rasping, hungry mouth between her legs.

MAUD BEGAN by escorting Cecile to the Paris ateliers, provisioning them with a wardrobe suitable for the warmer weather into which they were headed: dresses in light muslins and silks, their waists narrow, accented with a sash or belt, and wide-brimmed hats to keep off the sun, trimmed with ribbons and artificial flowers. Those adorned with exotic feathers, they ignored. Rancliffe, being firmly against the slaughtering of birdlife, would be enraged.

Afterwards, they lunched at the Café Anglais on the Grands Boulevards, ordering briny oysters and snails dripping in garlic-butter.

How stylish the French are, mused Cecile. *The women manage to look elegant even while eating with their fingers.*

In the evening, they ventured to Voisin, on the rue Saint-

Honoré, feasting on lobster thermidor and incomparable sole meunière, before taking their seats at a performance of Donizetti's *Lucrezia Borgia,* at the Paris Opera.

'A woman worthy of the name,' Maud whispered in Cecile's ear. 'Intelligent, *and* cunning.'

However, it seemed that cunning wasn't enough. Cecile couldn't help but wonder why women in such tales always came to a tragic end.

Does any opera end happily for the heroine? If I were to write the libretto, I'd ensure a better outcome. Surely, every woman's story doesn't need to end in misery.

The next day, after touring the Louvre, they drove down the Champs-Elysées, taking the air in Le Jardin des Tuileries. As in London, the parading of one's fashionableness was the prime intent.

At L'Arc de Triomphe, her brother insisted that Cecile have her portrait captured, a young man being ready with his photographic apparatus. Directed to stretch out her arms, as if pushing against the pillars of the arch, Cecile was aware of the eyes of passers-by upon her. Posing on the street was so very awkward.

Maud suggested that the man bring his equipment to the hotel one evening. 'I shall hire some oriental costumes and we shall play-act.' Her eyes were twinkling, Cecile noticed, with their customary mischief. 'A tableau, darling, don't you think? Just as you saw once, in London? We might capture the fun upon this gentleman's camera.'

Cecile turned away as her brother drew Maud to him and they engaged in the sort of kiss that, Cecile felt certain, was not seemly in public.

MAUD HAD INSISTED that Cecile be allowed to accompany them as much as possible, and be encouraged in new experiences.

They spent an evening at Le Café du Dôme, where the famous (and soon to be famous) ate plates of Saucisse de Tolouse and mashed potatoes for a few Francs. The room was thick with cigarette smoke, and with Bohemians: sculptors and painters, poets and writers. Models reclined on purple velvet banquettes, profiles displayed to advantage.

Another night, they dined at Maxim's on La Rue Royale, and drank absinthe at Le Casino de Paris, on la Rue de Clichy. 'Made from the flowers and leaves of *artemisia absinthium*, and sweet fennel,' Maud explained, stirring with a spoon and adding a little water.

Just like liquorice. Cecile sipped at the green liquid, and did her best not to show she didn't like it. Her brother kindly interceded, ordering her a glass of Calvados instead.

On a rainy Saturday evening, Cecile joined them at Les Folies-Bergère, her eyes widening at the sumptuous and grandiose spectacles, of acrobats and jugglers and fire-eaters, not to mention at the lack of clothing on the beautiful young women parading past.

'My goodness, they must be chilly!' she remarked, but Maud assured her that all the dancing kept them warm.

For comparison, they tried the Moulin Rouge, in the Jardin de Paris, with its red windmill on the roof and monumental elephant in the garden, around which tipsy revellers attempted the Can-Can, in emulation of the dancers in their titillating costumes.

Heavens! Cecile was quite flabbergasted. *Who'd have thought one's legs could do that!*

It was all diverting… though she couldn't help but wonder at the ostentatious artificiality of these amusements. Both evenings, she surveyed the audience, to see if she might recognize a certain tall gentleman with golden curls, but there was no sign of Lance. She was partly disappointed, but also relieved— not wanting to imagine him here, looking up the skirts of the audacious dancers.

On their fifth day, Cecile began to question whether she really liked the French capital at all.

Having ascended the Eiffel Tower and, marvelling at the view from the top, Cecile was startled to feel a hand grope at the underside of her bustle. She spun about, and the perpetrator, face impassive, faded into the crowd. By the time she found her voice, her assailant had truly disappeared.

What use will it do, now, to make a fuss? People will only think I'm drawing attention to myself, and it will be most distasteful.

Again, in the Basilique du Sacré-Cœur, on Montmatre, with Christ and all the saints and adorers looking down, her head cast upwards to take in the detail of the frescoed ceiling, Cecile found herself assaulted by a hefty pinch upon her *derrière*. This time, she turned to find no-one nearby but an elderly priest, clutching his prayer book.

He smiled benignly and walked on.

Europe, or what I've seen of it so far, is distinctly lacking in gallantry. By far the nicest man I've met is my Texan.

Except, of course, he was not *her* Texan.

If it had been love at first sight, Cecile lamented, *he would have torn off the edge of his map and written me a note, before we parted: some address, or a meeting place. Now, we shall never see each other again!*

Most likely, he was having adventures far away by now. The question was, what sort of adventures were in store for her? City life, though lively and surprising, was less engaging than she'd hoped, and filled with the unwanted press of other people.

Without much regret she waved off Maud and Henry on their penultimate evening in Paris, being content to take a light supper in her room, and spend time with the novel Maud had passed to her: a story by Mr Stoker, set in the dark mountains of Transylvania. An exciting read, Maud had promised, full of the mysterious unknown and unmapped landscapes.

'But don't tell your brother.' Leaving the edition on Cecile's dressing table, Maud had given a cloaked smile. 'He doesn't need to know everything.'

'REMEMBER,' Maud told Rancliffe, as they passed out of the doors of L'Hôtel Ritz, 'You're my escort, leading me by the hand as I indulge my wicked nature. Here to protect but not to subdue.'

'Of course, Mademoiselle.' He dropped his kiss upon her hand. 'Whatever amusements you seek, it's my pleasure to assist. Few men are so fortunate: to marry not one enchanting woman, but two.'

Maud laughed. 'We each possess more than a single face. Dig a little, and you'll find you've married a whole harem!'

Arm in arm, they explored the glittering streets of the moonlit city.

I'm in love, thought Rancliffe. *I thought I was before, and I was, but, now, it's something different.*

Sitting in a quiet corner booth, in la Brasserie de l'Espérance, on la rue Champollion, she twisted her fingers in the curls upon his collar, her eyes half-closed from too many glasses of champagne. 'What shall we do tonight, my husband? Shall we pay for some company?'

He stiffened in his seat, wary that they might be overheard, though the room was full of chatter.

Maud leant closer, her voice seductive. 'A soft mouthed woman, or one of your own sex? Someone strong?'

Rancliffe's mouth grew dry when she spoke like this. He remembered her as the taunting Mademoiselle Noire, appearing again to seduce and bewitch him. He shifted in his seat, lowering his eyes.

'Do you want hands that will be rough with you?' Her breath upon his ear made him shiver.

Rancliffe waved away the waiter, coming to refill their glasses.

'Someone to push you down, ordering you to kneel?' Maud's fingers deftly unbuttoned Rancliffe's trousers and she draped the edge of the tablecloth to conceal his lap.

Reaching inside, she encircled him, caressing his thickness in her palm. 'What will you do when your legs are pushed apart, when your lover enters you as if you were a woman? Will you beg to be taken deeper? Until you think you can bear no more? Until the final groan and judder?'

A few moments more and Rancliffe's cream covered her hand.

He did wish it, and he loved her for knowing.

WELL PAST MIDNIGHT, they headed to Le Chabanais, where the Prince of Wales had been known to spend an evening. In the Japanese room, where delicate bamboos and willows filled the pale green walls, Maud removed her evening gown of crimson silk and lay upon the bed's embroidered silk coverlet.

Rancliffe ached for her but his present role was only to watch: one girl after another, each given their turn to please his wife.

At last, her voice low and her eyes at their darkest, she said, 'Bring me a man.'

Not her husband.

Not him.

Not yet.

Nor an evening-suited diplomat or financier, though there were plenty of those to be found at this establishment.

It didn't take him long, just a few minutes' walk. He knew what she wanted. The man was as broad as a shire horse and provisioned, it turned out, with an organ worthy of the same; hair thick upon his chest and back, hands large as dinner plates, and breath reeking of cheap rum.

'I'm here to fuck you.' He staggered towards the bed, leering at her nakedness as he peeled off his braces, dropping his trousers to his ankles. He gave his meat a few tugs and, sneering, turned to Rancliffe. 'Not enough for her, eh? Needs a real man.'

Rancliffe made to rise from his seat, itching to give the blaggard a black eye, but Maud shook her head.

Laughing at Rancliffe's ire, the ruffian widened his stance and grasped Maud's legs, dragging her closer to the bed's edge. Gripping his erection, he lined himself up before making his thrust.

Maud's breath hitched and her lips parted, but her face remained impassive, as if in a trance.

Sliding his hands under her, the brute pulled Maud further onto his groin, so that only her shoulders and head remained upon the bed, her long hair flung behind. The man built a grunting rhythm.

A few minutes passed. 'What are yer like from behind?' said the Frenchman.

Turned downward, Maud's face was beside a golden hummingbird on the quilt. Her eyes were open, her head turned towards the chair Rancliffe sat upon, but he didn't think she saw him. Not now.

Maud had made herself clear. During these episodes, however self-destructive she might appear, he was not to intervene: only if her life were in danger, or if she summoned his help.

What drove her to such debasement?

Though, who was he to judge? Did he not have his own fantasies? Imaginings of couplings that he was too ashamed to share with anyone but Maud. Only she understood. Her tendency was to dominate, but there were times, like this, when her desire for submission, for humiliation, knew no bounds. Watching her, he saw another version of himself.

Nails sharp in his palms, he could hardly bear to look. At one word from Maud, he'd land a blow on the villain's nose. He'd boxed for his university club. He knew a thing or two.

Still, she did not speak.

Rancliffe looked away, but he could still hear: the man's heavy breathing, and the slap of his flesh against Maud's. Also, another sound. A soft, budding whimper. A plaintive cry.

Half-disgusted, half-aroused, Rancliffe turned back to see the man choke out his eruption, holding Maud rigid.

Afterwards, coughing from the exertion of his labours, the brute spat onto the rug. Wiping his nose on his sleeve, he pocketed the two Francs Rancliffe passed him.

3

Born with a substantial portion of Toscana in his pocket, the Conte di Cavour greeted the world with the appropriate level of condescension, and a readiness to take his amusement, regardless of the cost to others.

Gambling, whoring, drinking and hunting were his birthright; a legacy he cultivated with enthusiasm. In these pursuits, Lorenzo prided himself in setting the bar, since all men of nobility require an example before them. Even the Italian King, Umberto, in his younger years, had been inclined to accept an invitation from Lorenzo di Cavour.

From Siena to Milano to Venezia, he was notorious in his tastes, raising the painted eyebrows of even the most jaded prostitute.

No matter that, following a soirée to celebrate the fortieth anniversary of Lorenzo's birth, Signora Battaglia had been obliged to entirely redecorate her Yellow Salon—famed for its sumptuous décor, and furniture made by Francesco Scibec da Carpi (as graced the very chambers of Fontainebleau). The

evening had been a relatively civilized affair until a band of
female trapeze artists he'd befriended in Orvieto commenced
an innovative performance aided by four dozen champagne
corks and the salon's grand chandelier (itself a miniature of
those hanging in the Hall of Mirrors within the Palace of
Versailles).

The Conte had compensated Signora Battaglia so amply
that the good lady had commissioned a portrait in his honour,
which hangs still in the vestibule of that establishment.

Similarly, Signora Segreti had readily forgiven him for the
ruin of her collection of rare instruments of torture, extracted
from the Stanza di Tormenti, located beneath the Dominican
convent in Narni. Though restored by a blacksmith, they
would never be as they were. Of course, everyone agreed that
the cheerfully compliant contortionist duo of Esmeralda and
Eduardo should, in truth, be apportioned some share of the
blame.

Lorenzo was seldom fully sober, but when he was, the glint
in his cold, dark eyes fixed in earnest upon his prey. It was
then that his wolf-gaze was at its most dangerous. He was a
fallen angel, as devoid of remorse or conscience as Satan
himself.

One might have called him the epitome of honesty, since he
made no attempt to conceal his sins. His scandals, each more
outrageous than the next, appeared with regularity in the
provincial newspapers, and, on occasion, in journals of
international circulation. His exploits, being always worthy of
report, might have occupied every edition, but that the
wealthier victims of his debauchery oft bribed silence from
those who would make public their shame.

The greediest of matrons, eager for their debutante daughters to marry into wealth and position, yet baulked at placing
their tender offspring in his path. How many fair lilies had

been plucked from under the noses of the unwary? Having cast his carnal spell, even the most demure allowed him liberties.

The pursuit of a trembling virgin, aquiver with anticipation and fear, would occupy him for an hour. It amused him to recall those gasps at the pinching of an inner thigh, and the straying of his fingers to places untouched even by the lady in question.

How many pretty necks had his teeth grazed, as his thumb delved and teased? Arms curled about his neck and legs parted in eager invitation, pulling him close while decrying his damnable audacity.

None returned to her Mama quite the same. Skirts and hair could be smoothed, and faces composed, but each young "figlia" tottered back to her chaperone with new knowledge and a spirit of defiance.

It was his gift to them.

A firm hand cannot be denied, and his was a hand of experience: of pleasure and pain, and all that lay between.

Of course, there was far more satisfaction in seducing a woman whose outward show of respectability crumbled under his tutelage. Many a wife had he sent home to her husband with the sting of his palm or his crop upon her buttocks, her flesh smarting, yet thrilling at the humiliation.

It amused him to see how far he could push their sensibilities and, as a thoughtful master, he ensured his man, Serpico, a share in the fun.

On a recent trip to visit his mother at her London house, he and Serpico had enjoyed the company of Baroness Billington and her sister, aided by three dock labourers Serpico collected on his nocturnal wanderings. Lorenzo had been quite tempted to send the ladies on their way, at the sight of those firm and muscular chests, and biceps handsomely inked. His own knees weakened when presented with so much glorious cock. The remembrance still made his balls ache.

Naturally, life could not always be filled with frivolous pleasure. There were occasional slights to be avenged, for which he was obliged to set aside his good humour. Lorenzo did not lack imagination, and Serpico ensured that none escaped their due.

On that count, one score remained unsettled, though not forgotten. A certain young woman under his mother's protection might think she'd bested him, but his memory was long. A day would come when she would rue her clever games. Until then, he had time enough to plan…

PADRE GIOVANNI, of the small town of Pietrocina, had spent a lifetime cultivating his belief in the fiery flames of Hell, warning with all due urgency of the torments that awaited those indulging in ungodly acts.

Corruption of the flesh he renounced with particular rigour, studying his female flock closely, that he might better identify those cast upon temptation's path, and insist on every detail via the confessional.

His housekeeper, Maria Boerio, stout of figure and of constitution, had served him ably over the years. Each morning, she checked upon him, to reassure herself that her Beloved Padre, for such he was to her, breathed still.

In his slumber, she admired the less weary appearance of his face, and traced the now sagging line of his jaw, the stubble accumulated through the night. That she oft contemplated stealing a kiss was her greatest secret. No matter that his eyes were cloudy, and his nasal hair grew more abundant with the passing years, or that she knew the state of his bowels by the condition of the undergarments she scrubbed. To her, he was all that a man should be: serious-minded and above earthly temptations.

Like most men of his age, he was prone to piles. Even in this, she did her best to soothe him, preparing a tea of butcher's broom, and an ointment of witch hazel and camomile. If he were to request the application of the unguent to the pale recesses of his behind, she would do so without question. Sadly, such a plea had never been voiced.

Though it was a shameful sin, she had, at times, hidden where she might spy upon him, wishing to behold that dear, though aged, body, in its naked splendour. Enfeebled as it was, the elbows and knees at sharp angles, and the stomach flabby, to Maria, the padre's form was a vision.

Her peeping had afforded her, just once, the sight of his penis: a sad, flaccid little thing barely worthy of the name. She'd pictured coaxing it to life and guiding it, to offer the ultimate comfort.

Such wicked imaginings could not always be avoided, but his purity was her comfort, as she told herself, her hand cupping that place of warmth betwixt ample thighs. How fortunate that the padre was a man of God, and above such dissolute thoughts.

LEAVING Serpico to follow on with the bulk of his luggage, the Conte Lorenzo di Cavour took a train from Pisa, through Roma, and onto Napoli, before boarding a coach. This conveyed him to Sorrento by late afternoon. He might have taken a room at the Paradiso Vigoria, to enjoy its lush gardens of citrus and olive groves, looking out over the azure expanse of the bay. In all likelihood, the chambermaids would have obliged him in some amusing manner. He had entertained himself there often enough before.

However, he was eager to reach his destination, the Castello di Scogliera. With the sun dipping into the final quarter of the sky, Lorenzo boarded a carriage heading to Salerno, via Scogliera and Pietrocina. Already inside sat an elderly priest: an unappealing specimen, to the conte's eyes. However, he nodded in greeting and smiled to himself. He'd anticipated sharing the carriage with at least one other passenger, and this white-haired man of the cloth, snuffling into his pocket-handkerchief, would suit admirably. Fate would now watch over their journey, if not God (whom Lorenzo had long been convinced looked the other way, if He looked at all).

A few minutes later, the door opened again, hailing the entrance of a third to join them: a woman dressed head to toe in black, gloved, veiled and hatted. Settling herself on the cushions opposite, she spread her skirts as best she might in the confined spot. There was little space between them. Their knees would touch were Lorenzo to slouch a few inches. She held her head erect and, though masked by her veil, he would have wagered 10,000 liras that her look was one of indignation and of challenge; even, contempt.

The driver placing his whip to the horses, the carriage jolted and swayed, and they moved across the cobbles of the Piazza Tasso, towards the Via Fuorimura, and southwards, past the street-sellers and the first evening promenaders.

Padre Giovanni Gargiullo shifted uncomfortably. His hemorrhoids were paining him more than usual—perhaps due to the heat. Returning from his summons to Sorrento by Bishop Cavicchioni, his report on the declining number of faithful attending Mass had not been well received. The Bishop had pointed out that not all could be suffering from malady, and the residents of his small town produced children enough to compensate for those who shuffled off this mortal coil. Padre Gargiullo was out of favour, and would not be invited to attend the Bishop's anniversary celebrations; nor would he be granted a bonus to his stipend.

Feeling thus sorry for himself, he sought consolation in his

Bible, opening his favourite passage, in Galatians: '*Now the works of the flesh are manifest, which are: adultery, fornication, uncleanness, lasciviousness...*'

As they passed the outskirts of the town, gaining a clearer view of the rugged mountain tops ahead, the conte was the first to speak.

'How warm it is this evening. You'll permit me to open the window? Perhaps the dusk air will refresh us.' Without waiting for a reply, he leant over and did just that, allowing the coolness to enter in.

Padre Giovanni looked up from his Bible, ready to offer thanks for this consideration, but the words died in his throat.

The gentlewoman, sitting so daintily and decorously, had loosened the buttons at her neck. Not two or three, but six or seven, such that the jacket of her costume had fallen open almost to her navel. Beneath, where her blouse should have been, it was not. Nor was there chemise, nor camisole, nor corset.

The padre's instinct was to cry out, to voice his alarm, to rage at her indecency. His lips moved to shape his protest and yet...not a sound emerged.

Her skin was smooth.

Unblemished.

He could not look away.

Reaching for the pins at the back of her coiffure, she removed one. A single coil of curled ebony fell free.

With her eyes upon the clergyman, she moved the fabric of her jacket to one side, to expose fully the sweet roundness of her breast. Such softness, and youth: her areola the palest pink, and large. Her gloved hand cupped her flesh: displaying, offering, inviting. Her hair brushed the nipple: satin against silk, midnight against moonlight.

A squeeze rendered the peak pert.

The conte was tempted to utter some word of admiration or encouragement, but held his tongue.

Padre Giovanni was incapable of speaking, his mouth having turned quite dry. His fingers clutched at his Bible. Several of the pages had crumpled rather badly.

The lady leant forward, her breasts swinging free of her jacket, bending until she grasped the hem of her skirts. Inch by inch, the taffeta and muslin rose above the ankle of her boot. She paused at her knee, her eyes flicking to the conte, assuring herself that he observed her still.

His mouth twitched a little, as if he might at any moment laugh.

The lady wore no undergarments.

As the top of her stockings were revealed, the padre's fingers fluttered against his book, losing their grip. The volume fell to the floor with a thump, its corner catching his smallest toe, extracting a yelp.

Parting her thighs, the lady pulled her skirts entirely upwards. There, at last, was the moist fur between her legs.

The padre's voice emerged in a squeak.

Lorenzo, meanwhile, permitted himself a slight shift in his seat, tugging his britches into greater comfort.

She removed a single glove. Unfastening its buttons, she tugged, until her elegant fingers were free. The lady stretched her hand, as if it were a cat's paw, the claws of which required extension.

With all languor, she found the slickness between her legs and, arching back, her jacket fell fully open. Her breasts pushed upwards, and her nipples stiffened under the gaze of the two men sitting so very close.

Legs parted, labia parted, her secret self parted, she folded back that wild and wicked rose, to reveal its darkest recesses.

Here I am, she declared silently. *Here is all there is to see. Here is what men desire: the essence of womanhood, from which all life springs. Look and admire.*

The padre felt himself both ice and fire: a pillar of salt and of water. With certainty, he could no longer feel his legs.

The lady's head lolled back. She rocked against her fingers, first slow and then harder, her breasts rising and falling with her quickening breath. Hips writhing, a wrathful snake was uncoiling, traveling through womb, belly and spine—and then snake became raven, taking off in flight. Her voice a wail, she flung off the trappings of her imprisoned humanity, becoming one with the air and the night.

Time stopped for some moments, though not one of the three could measure them.

Lorenzo had to admit, she'd surpassed herself, and he'd witnessed some performances in his time.

'Brava, Lucrezia dear.' He raised his hands in applause. 'I should have known better than to throw down such an enticing challenge to one so talented.'

The lady fumbled with her buttons, her fingers somewhat trembling from the feverish flood bathing her body.

'I'm sure I speak not only for myself but for our good padre in offering you my heartfelt admiration,' continued the conte. 'How unfortunate it is that we're almost at our destination, for I feel certain that a second act would have proven most welcome. A good hard fuck does one the world of good, and the padre looks rather in need of a tonic. A rough poke of your delightful cunt, my dear, would have revived him no end.'

Padre Giovanni's eyes blazed, his mouth working to express his outrage, but the appropriate words failed him.

Her locks re-pinned, Lucrezia threw down her skirts and turned to face the clergyman.

'Take no notice of my half-brother's crude taunts, Padre,' she soothed. 'He's a child you know, always eager for novelty. I imagine that you, more than he, appreciate the true revelation of a woman's passion: a flame lit by Divine God himself, and placed within exquisite flesh, to His own design.'

Having arrived in Scogliera, the two left Padre Giovanni in peace.

To his shame, the padre's lap was damp.

4

WITHIN THE CASTELLO DI SCOGLIERA, two sat by candlelight.

The woman's eyes were strangely bright, as if the twinkling crystals of the chandelier above the dining table had dropped into those dark pools. Raising her glass, she drank deeply. 'Do you have a conscience, brother? Or were you born without the capacity to feel guilt, or shame?'

'You know me better than anyone, sister dear. If you say it's so, I must believe you.' Lorenzo raised his glass to hers.

'I'd declare you the blackest villain, were it not for your occasional softness towards those of your own blood. The paradox is that you derive such pleasure from tormenting us.'

'My dear Lucrezia, what form would your rebellion take, had you not my little cages to rail against? I merely feed your desire to disobey.'

The matter of their argument was for the moment set aside, as Vittoria entered, bringing with her the chocolate tartufo.

'A letter arrived this afternoon, sister, from dear Aunt Agatha. Having invited her grand-daughter to spend her honeymoon at the villa, she requests a room with us for a few weeks, to allow the newlyweds their fun.'

Lucrezia paused. 'The renowned beauty, who was staying with your mother—in London?'

Lorenzo's knife sliced into the tartufo.

'A handsome marriage to a young aristocrat, I hear...' Lucrezia added.

Lorenzo waved his hand in dismissal. 'My time in London was brief. I barely spoke to the lady in question. She was tolerably attractive, though I fear will not age well.'

'I wonder at your forgetting her so easily,' asserted Lucrezia. 'A little bird told me that Isabella hoped this pretty thing might ensnare you.'

'I do not say that I forget.' Lorenzo's eyes narrowed. 'Agatha requests accommodation for the groom's sister also, a girl barely presented to Society. No doubt, she will be a bore, with no conversation or other talent to recommend her. I must leave her to you Lucrezia. Your tolerance for dullness exceeds my own.'

Finding the cherries within the tartufo, Lorenzo bit down upon them. The stain of scarlet syrup spread upon his lips.

'As you wish.' Lucrezia held his gaze. 'But I must be rewarded. I've kept my side of too many bargains, and I'm yet to see the benefit.'

Lorenzo licked his spoon thoughtfully. 'I'm listening, though you're hardly in a position to make demands of me.'

'You know perfectly well what I want,' hissed Lucrezia, her fists clenched tight upon the table. 'A larger income, so that I might make my own way, and leave here. Away from you!'

'The money is easily arranged.' Lorenzo gave a wolfish smile. 'But you would miss me, would you not?'

Lucrezia, for once in command of her temper, declined to answer.

'Perhaps we might play a game, to while away the tedium of

entertaining our young houseguest. My aunt, I know, will amuse herself, but young women are so… needy.'

Lucrezia knew Lorenzo's games of old.

'I wonder, sister dear, which of us might first make a conquest of this squeaking mouse. Show me the little pet, tamed and compliant in your paw, and I will fulfil your request: an allowance of a million Lira a year, in whichever currency you prefer.'

He allowed the sum to hang before Lucrezia, laden with possibilities. 'If her soft fur finds its way between my teeth, I'll devise an amusement of my own choosing, to which I will expect you to comply.'

Lucrezia grew a little pale. There were few things she denied Lorenzo, grateful to him for having claimed her, his half-blood, from the orphanage in which she was raised, but she was wise to the paths of his cunning.

'I know how well you rise to a challenge. Your performance for the padre passed the carriage journey most pleasurably. You have a talent for play-acting, like your mother before you. Sleep on it, my Lucrezia.' He spooned the last of the dessert into his mouth. 'And may your dreams be sweet.'

LUCREZIA REMOVED the rubies from her ears, and fingered the expensive bottles upon her dressing table. Her brother had been generous but the price was too high. All under his roof were his to command and the yoke was becoming heavier. His torment, devising new ways in which she must bend herself to accommodate his whim, was insufferable.

The fate of the young woman soon to join them was nothing to her. What did she care for some spoilt and silly English girl, who could not begin to imagine the life Lucrezia had endured. It would be easy enough to win her trust. She'd extract a kiss from her within a week.

Harder would be the task of keeping her girlish fancies from Lorenzo's roguish charm. Liberally applied, it rarely failed.

She envisioned well the forfeit she'd pay if he won this wager: the one thing she had refused him, though not on grounds of morality or fear of the Almighty.

She would never offer that part of herself. No man would have her so utterly in his power.

SITTING ALONE AT THE TABLE, Lorenzo clicked his fingers and, from the shadows, a dark figure emerged.

'I have unfinished business with the new countess. We'll bide our time, but —be ready to act when the opportunity presents itself. Go to the villa, Serpico. Watch, and listen.'

5

FROM PARIS, they travelled to Strasbourg, onwards to Munich, then Prague, and southwards to Vienna, until they reached the darkly mysterious Budapest, where Gothic turrets and Baroque palaces vie with Byzantine architecture.

Cecile was enchanted by the Hungarian capital. Here, at last, was a sense of inscrutability: the presence of the past, of interwoven centuries, offering glimpses of their secrets.

The weather grew warmer as the weeks passed, and they ventured further south.

Cecile lost count of how many galleries and museums she visited, how many cathedrals. It astonished her that so many churches were filled with the voluptuous. Paintings and sculpture of earthly flesh, in close proximity with the divine. There was something compelling in those outstretched hands, reaching upwards to the Heavens. Hands of sinners and saints, seeking something beyond themselves.

Finally, they headed towards Italy, via Zagreb. In Venice, a gondola brought them down the Grand Canal, and through the maze of smaller waterways. They visited the gilded Palace of Ca' d'Oro, with its courtyard of ancient marbles and ornate balconies, then toured the Doge's Palace. As the sun lowered to the last quadrant, they took a table at a café in Piazza San Marco, drinking coffee and watching passers-by: young men walking out with their sweethearts; mothers shepherding their children, who threw breadcrumbs to the birds; grandmothers selling posies of flowers from brimming baskets.

Maud pointed out a pickpocket in the crowd, one she'd seen sidling up to people in the throng. 'He brushes against them as lightly as an insect pollinating a flower, taking what he needs, while leaving nothing in return but the promise of dismay.' She sipped from her cup of rich, dark coffee.

'How dreadful,' exclaimed Cecile. 'We should alert the *polizia!*'

She was a little testy; so many hands, always reaching to touch her, to stroke the white-blonde of her hair, to take some ownership of her person. She was irritated by old women presuming to pinch her cheek, so fair in comparison to the olive tones of Southern European skin.

In truth, Cecile was dissatisfied with herself. She'd hoped to feel changed by these travels, to have her mind opened. Instead, one city seemed much like another. They each had their monuments and their beauties but everywhere was the same congregation, the same grasping, pressing confluence.

'Everyone must make their living, as best they can.' Maud shrugged.

Cecile looked to her brother for his opinion, but he kept his eyes on his copy of Baedeker's *Handbook for Travellers.* She was left to fume in silence.

Maud and Henry continued to include Cecile in their excursions, and her every comfort was accommodated, yet she felt a strange discomfort—a sense of exclusion that had grown with the passing weeks. Her brother was content in his marriage, she was sure. Yet, at times, there was something feverish about him.

Having read in a story by Mr Doyle about Sherlock Holmes, and his addiction to opium, she wondered if her brother had fallen into the habit. Once, waking in the small hours, hearing him and Maud return from some entertainment, she'd knocked on their connecting door. Henry, opening it to her, was so unlike himself, eyes huge and dark in his pale face.

Some unknown force sat between them, separating her from Henry, and from his bride. She'd hoped to become closer to Maud during their travels but their rekindled friendship, in London, seemed an age away. Maud, now a wife, and privy to things Cecile could not imagine, occupied another universe. Maud's affinity towards Claudette, her new maid, hired in Paris, seemed closer than that towards Cecile, her own sister-in-law.

All things change. Perhaps, one day, when I'm married and wise, I shall look back on myself, and not recognize the girl I was.

Cecile joined her brother and Maud in taking a *vaporetti* across the viridian waters of the Venice lagoon, to the isle of Murano, where Henry ordered fifteen chandeliers of hand-blown glass, each tiny crystal droplet threaded with gold, for delivery to his London residence.

'So many, my love?' commented Maud. 'We've barely four reception rooms at Eaton Square.'

'Ah, but we shall need something larger, shall we not. A married man requires a grander home; there must be space for children.'

Maud's lips formed a thin line. 'How many are you hoping for?'

'One to start with.' Henry answered quietly, dropping a kiss upon her glove.

Cecile's cheeks grew warm at this mention of private

matters. She was feeling, more than ever, that to live as a suppliant under the roof of her brother and his wife was a state she could not long endure. She was the gooseberry, set against their wedded ease. As kind as Henry and Maud had been, her place was untenable.

What choices did she have?

Marriage to someone 'sensible', of her brother's choosing? Or spinsterhood, living with her aunt, in Oxfordshire?

Both visions made her shudder.

Her daydreams of emulating the noble Ms McTavish, in her exploration of the wild territories, were no more than flights of fancy. Her spirit was willing, but the practicalities were beyond her—even were Henry to release funds to indulge such travel. Her own pocket-book income was too small to conceive of true independence.

She must marry. There was no way around it. But where were the suitors of her star-gazing? Where was her brave soldier? Her dashing prince? Her noble knight?

As they sat at breakfast in the dining car, Rancliffe hungrily consuming kedgeree, Maud sipped from her teacup, looking at the passing countryside, the terrain growing more mountainous.

How many trains had they taken since leaving Paris, slicing through the miles and the hours, by day and night?

She was thinking of her husband's lovemaking, moving in syncopation with the engine's forward motion and the rhythmic rocking of their carriage. Rancliffe staring intently into her face, his fingers in her hair, wrapped around her, inside and out, flying through the dark.

His kisses were most often reverential—like those of an angel kissing the hand of God—but they could be something else too. She preferred the latter. Rancliffe was apt to be tender, when what she needed was something else.

Most nights, Maud lay awake, watching her husband sleep, just as she knew he watched her in the morning. His face was noble in repose, eyelids fluttering as he dreamt.

She dreamt too. The ghosts of the departed sat still upon her bed. She'd hoped they'd move a little further off, now that she was married. Perhaps they would, eventually.

Beneath the table, she kicked off her slipper and touched her stockinged foot to his leg, eliciting a smile from her husband.

Cecile, sitting beside her brother, began to make conversation on the weather, speculating on how hot it might become. Pointedly, she turned her face to the window.

We've been discreet... or discreet enough, Maud thought. *It's too tiresome to be always checking my behaviour, and with my own husband! Really, it will be as well when Cecile has a husband and home of her own.*

THEY TRAVELLED SOUTH, to the marvels of Florence. After trips to Pisa and medieval Siena, they reached Rome, and the sultry heat of Naples. The summer had arrived in earnest, the midday heat obliging them to make early morning excursions to view glowering Vesuvio and the ruins of Pompeii.

They arrived in Sorrento on the late afternoon train to a carriage sent by Maud's grandmother. They progressed slowly, up the winding coastal path, under hanging trees, as the sun relinquished its hold on the day. Cliffs loomed above as they climbed, the rock face closing in as they journeyed higher.

The carriage continued through the dwindling light, navigating the twists of the road until their heads nodded sleepily. After some time, a jolt woke Cecile and she looked down from the window, down the steep cliff face, down to the waves below.

The moon had risen, emerging through rolling, black clouds to reveal a brooding silhouette of a castle, perched high upon an island of rock in the centre of the bay. Its jagged turrets were too numerous to count, but one dominated all.

From that dark pinnacle amid the vast, inscrutable sea, a light winked, as if calling to her.

6

Lady Agatha Courcy, Maud's grandmother, had intuited that the lovebirds would welcome some time alone.

All was arranged with her nephew, whose home—the ancient seat of the di Cavour dynasty—lay but four miles away. After a week of merriment at the villa, Cecile joined Agatha in her carriage, clattering across the cobbles of the causeway, towards the island in the bay.

Ahead were those towering turrets, the same as had whispered to Cecile on the night of her arrival, their narrow windows catching the morning sun, glinting like so many eyes, looking down upon those who approached.

Sitting beside her elderly companion, Cecile felt again an uncanny tug, somewhere beneath her ribcage, as if an invisible thread were attached there, drawing her, inevitably, closer.

They passed beneath a mighty arch, onwards, up a steep track, barely wide enough to admit them. The horses plodded their ascent through lush foliage, the wheels of the carriage skimming nodding lilies. Branches of oleander brushed the roof.

At last, the path opened, and the horses stopped before the great doors of the castle itself.

Through the surrounding cyprus trees, the Mediterranean could be glimpsed, stretching onward: a shimmering vision.

'*Benvenuto!*' called a voice.

'*Mia cara! Bello per vederti. Come va?*' replied Agatha.

'*Molto bene, grazie,*' answered the dark-haired beauty emerging from the castle. She wasted no time in embracing them both, clasping her arms about Cecile as if they'd known each other always. '*Benvenuto, nuova amica.*'

'Oh! Good morning!' Cecile smiled shyly. 'It's lovely to meet you. But I'm afraid I really don't speak Italian.'

'Ah!' The young woman surveyed Cecile with a twinkling eye. 'But now you are here, in our *bella Italia,* you will learn.'

'Really, Lucrezia! You must know that it's too forward to jump upon a new acquaintance,' berated Agatha. 'Cecile won't know what to make of you!'

'*Scusami.*' Lucrezia dropped a flamboyant curtsy. 'You will learn Italian, Cecile, and perhaps I will learn manners.'

'Impossible girl!' Agatha shook her head.

'I shall improve myself,' promised Lucrezia, bestowing Agatha with a kiss upon both cheeks. '*Adesso!* Let us go in, and take the English tea.'

CECILE'S CHAMBER was quite charming. Beside her hearth was a small chaise, upholstered in golden yellow damask, and near the window a dainty writing desk.

Draped in white muslin embroidered with honeysuckle, the bed was carved with all manner of creatures: frogs and beetles and birds nestled between creeping ivy, curling about the bedposts.

'Like fingers about a lover's neck, yes?' Lucrezia traced a tendril of wooden ivy upon the polished surface.

Cecile nodded in mute assent. What things Lucrezia said! And how she dressed!

Lucrezia's day-gown, like Cecile's, was made from fine cotton, but the cut was far more daring, revealing the swell of her ample bosom. A design of interwoven snakes encircled her waist, created from tiny beads, in all shades of green.

'I sewed this belt,' said Lucrezia, proudly, seeing Cecile's eyes upon her costume. 'The serpent is an emblem of the di Cavours.'

She flicked out her tongue and gave a playful hiss, laughing to see Cecile's startled expression. 'Do not worry, *mia cara*. I promise only to lead you into pleasant temptations.'

Cecile turned away, not knowing what to say.

Nothing was as she'd imagined it might be—neither stark nor dingy. The dust and cobwebs of past generations did not hang from the bedstead. Rather, dazzling sun pushed through the window, the shutters of which were folded back.

Below was the terrace and the slope of the garden, exquisitely lush, leading down, out of sight. Beyond was an expanse of blue, the water mirroring the undisturbed azure of the heavens.

From the pale-wash upon the wooden floors, to the white pillows and linens, brightness filled the room. The walls too were painted white, though far from bare. A garden of butterflies, thick among bougainvillea, had been conjured upon them, fluttering beside berry-eating birds. 'You should see the jungle in my room, with tigers! But this gentle garden I made for you.'

'It's marvellous! How clever you are!' Cecile had spent many hours with a paintbrush and canvas, under the guiding eye of the art master at the Beaulieu Academy for Ladies. Never had she created anything a fraction as magical.

On impulse, she traversed the few steps between them and gathered Lucrezia in an embrace. One of gratitude, but something else too—a feeling of kinship. For, despite the luxuries with which Lucrezia was surrounded, was she not alone, just as Cecile found herself to be? Did she seek a soulmate, someone she could trust?

'Come.' Lucrezia tugged Cecile's hand. 'We must show you, now, a real Italian *giardino*.'

'WE HAVE SOMETHING IN COMMON, you and I,' said Lucretia.

They descended, skirts brushing dahlias as large as saucers, cheerful marigolds, and the fat heads of peonies, following steps cut into the granite upon which the castle stood. Insects flitted back and forth, dipping into brimming cups of pollen.

Cecile pressed her handkerchief to her forehead. The day was blazing and she'd forgotten her hat. Fortunately, as the path wound down, they entered the shade of a pergola, tumbling with a profusion of jasmine and hanging clusters of wisteria.

'I'm sure we have many things in common.' Cecile stooped to inhale the scent of a pink rose, unfurled to its full-blown beauty. 'A wish to discover more about the world, to explore new places, and to find true love, of course, and our place in Society.'

Lucrezia plucked the head from a lily, resting the powdered stamen against her chin, where it left a yellow stain. 'Perhaps. But I was thinking more of the past than the future. She paused. 'Agatha told me you lost your mother, long ago.'

It was not a subject upon which Cecile chose to dwell. She wasn't alone in suffering loss, and there was nothing to gain from pitying oneself. Maud certainly did not.

Cecile, at least, had Henry. Although...

It occured to her that he was more Maud's than hers these days.

'Forgive me.' Lucrezia placed a hand on Cecile's arm. 'I do not wish to stir unwanted memories, only to tell you of myself, since we shall be friends in this place. I, too, am without a mother's guidance.'

Cecile realized she'd been frowning, which wouldn't do at all. 'I didn't mean to be rude. You lost your mother, too? Please, tell me of her, if it doesn't pain you.'

'It is a sad tale but you will be a patient listener, I can tell.' Sitting upon a stone bench within the arbour, Lucrezia tapped beside her, encouraging Cecile to rest also.

'She was one of Milan's most celebrated *Diva Operativa*. No one sang Violetta in Verdi's *La Traviata* better than she. The old conte, Camillo, pursued her, and won her in all respects, though she was no more than a dalliance for him. By the time I was born, her heart was broken.'

Lucrezia gazed upon the lily she held, twirling it slowly. 'She placed me in an orphanage, writing to Camillo to tell him of my whereabouts, then threw herself from the roof of La Scala.' With those last words, Lucrezia let the flower fall from her fingers.

Cecile cried in horror. 'Oh, Lucrezia!'

'A lesson to all young women, I would say.' Lucrezia gave a brittle laugh. 'To his credit, my father paid generously to ensure that I was never ill-treated. Nevertheless, his interest extended no further than to read an annual report of my continued presence in the world. It was upon his death that Lorenzo sought me out, and brought me to live with him, though his mother, Isabella, was less than delighted.'

'Such a tragic story.' Cecile sniffed a little.

'When I think of her—my mother—I imagine she's in another room.' Lucrezia paused.

Had Cecile been paying more attention she might have

noticed her new friend pinching the underside of her wrist sufficiently to make her eyes water.

'A locked door separates us. Except that, one day, the door won't be locked anymore...' Lucrezia gave a heartfelt sigh.

The two sat quietly for a moment.

'And what of you? Tell me of your mother.' Beckoning Cecile to walk again, Lucrezia led them into a flood of sunlight, to a clear view over the sea. On all sides was an abundance of lavender and camomile, threaded with purple irises and wild garlic. Thyme pushed up between the flagstones. Piled in happy heaps and jumbles, the garden was perfect in its chaos, the salt-scented breeze a top note over the mixed fragrance of a thousand blooms.

'I was so young when she died, of influenza. I don't recollect much about her, but I do wonder what it would have been like if she'd lived; she and my father,' said Cecile.

Lucrezia, though curious, knew there was a limit to how far she might politely probe. Cecile would tell her what was pertinent in her own time. Diplomacy was the best strategy, coupled with a tone of intimacy.

As if struck by a blinding notion, she declared. 'We have been sent to one other! You and I shall be sisters!'

And, though Cecile had known Lucrezia only a short time, her heart leapt. Everything in Scogliera was so vibrant, so colourful and lively.

She was seized with a rush of emotion. 'You can't know, really, how I've longed for a sister. I thought, perhaps, that Maud might... but I can't seem to know her properly. I don't think she ever tells me, truly, how she's feeling.'

Lucrezia slipped her arm through Cecile's. 'Maud is a married woman, with other preoccupations than our own. But we understand each other, *mia sorella*, and we shall begin by telling our secrets.'

'Oh! That won't take long at all. I've never done much of anything worth keeping secret.'

'Whereas, I have a great many.' Lucrezia grinned.

Cecile gave her arm a companionable squeeze. 'I might have to make some up, or you'll think me terribly dull.'

Lucrezia was obliged to turn her head, that her face might not betray her. How completely without guile the child was!

'I love the wildness of this garden,' proclaimed Cecile. 'The wisteria, tumbling as it likes, and the roses. So much untamed beauty. I hardly know where to look first, and everything framed by this never-ending sky and the open waters stretching away.'

Lucrezia nodded. 'It is free in a way that we are not. Perhaps that is why it inspires us, yes?'

'Oh! I've a great many freedoms.' Cecile brushed her palm against a swathe of daisies, their faces filled with the sun. 'My brother's very generous, and more forward-thinking than most men, I'm sure. In London, I attended meetings of the National Union of Women's Suffrage Societies, with Maud. Rancliffe's a great believer in women having their own voice.'

'I am delighted to hear it.' Lucrezia swatted her hand against the same blooms. 'I fear we are not so far ahead. A woman has no voice unless she is married, and then her voice is that of her husband, rather than herself. Even our clothes are designed to rein us in—as if our bodies were something to be feared!'

They continued down, each set of steps leading to a lower terrace, past arches overgrown with wandering vines and trailing passionflowers, and the sweet, thick breath of jasmine. The path tumbled with scarlet geraniums and blazing nasturtiums.

'But we couldn't not wear them, could we—our corsets, I mean.' mused Cecile.

'Let us take a stand,' countered Lucrezia. 'Think how lovely it will be to have your muslin chemise against your skin, and nothing else.'

'It *is* hot.' Cecile's voice was hopeful.

Lucrezia twisted a peach from its stem, taking a bite, letting the juice run down her fingers. 'From tomorrow, no more corsets.'

Already, Lucrezia was imagining her constriction lifting: liberated not only from her tiresome stays but from the confinement of Lorenzo's domination.

Why should she not win the wager he'd thrown down?

PASSING the citrus-sharp tang of lemon trees and branches laden with ripening cherries, they came to the water's edge.

There, they sat for some time, perched on the smoothest of the rocks, petticoats tucked up. The tide was at its highest, and most still. A serene warmth embraced them.

Cecile wiggled her toes in the lapping waves. 'Do you ever sail from here?'

'Sadly not. No boat can be launched, as the rocks are so jagged. They hide beneath the water's surface.'

'Ah yes, a concealed danger.' Cecile tilted back her head to the sun. 'Waiting to shipwreck the unwary.'

'*Sì, mia piccolo.*' Lucrezia's answer was quietly spoken.

At last, they moved to the shade of the terrace above and, tucked under an olive tree, they ate more peaches. Had Cecile ever been so happy?

This is what a garden must look like when it's consumed centuries of warmth. It's nothing like the Castle of Otranto, or Udolpho. There's nothing sinister here. Only sunshine and happiness.

As if in agreement came the sound of cheerful whistling.

'Who's that?' asked Cecile, casting her eyes towards the branches of a tree not far off. Someone had climbed there, to better cut a crossed branch, and perhaps to admire the view, which was particularly lovely on that summer's day.

'Raphael.' Lucrezia lay with her arm across her brow but she didn't need to look. 'Our gardener; Piero, is too old now to manage on his own. Raphael is his grandson. He looks after Agatha's gardens, too. He is most obliging; will do anything you ask. Anything at all…'

'Your gardens must need a lot of watering.'

'Sì, lots… Every day is ideal. Twice sometimes.' Lucrezia rolled onto her side, twitching a grass stem between her teeth.

The two fell into quiet contemplation, although their thoughts did not, perhaps, follow quite the same path.

'And now I ask you the question most intimate…' Lucrezia raised herself upon her elbow, choosing her next arrow with care. 'Do you ever wonder what it is like to join in passion with a man?'

'Lucrezia!' Cecile sat up in surprise. 'What a thing to say!'

'Not Raphael of course,' added her Italian friend. 'That would be not right at all, would it?'

'I should think not.' However, Cecile was looking at the strong arms of that young man, who was wielding his saw with great mastery.

'I mean to say, I wonder what it must be like when you are married,' said Lucrezia.

It was the sort of topic one wasn't meant to think about, let alone discuss, but Cecile found herself wanting to appear a little worldly. 'Well, I do know a little.'

'Do you truly?' Lucrezia sat up herself, giving Cecile all her attention. 'Then, I must beg you to share your knowledge. It would shame me to admit the extent of my innocence.'

Cecile lowered her eyes, warmth filling her cheeks, now that she was obliged to elaborate. 'I've heard that, when a wife embraces her husband, there's a little bell inside of her that starts to ring, just like the one inside a church tower. But smaller of course.'

'A bell?' Lucrezia gave a bark of laughter which she quickly converted to a sneeze. '*Scusami!* It's the pollen, *cara.* Only the pollen.'

'Oh! I've a handkerchief in my pocket.' Cecile drew it out. 'It was in the drawer beside my bed. Perhaps it's one of yours?'

Unfolding the linen, Lucrezia fingered the elaborately embroidered monogram of the letter "L", and there was no more merriment in her expression.

'Ah yes, possibly. Though the castle has seen many guests in its time. It could belong to… anyone.'

7

'I HOPE you find yourself comfortable, Lady McCaulay,' the conte enquired, as they sat to dine. 'And that our little piece of Italy agrees with you. We enjoy the isolated splendour of our island, but we sadly lack many of the modern comforts of this age. We do without electricity, we wrap ourselves against draughts, and live with floors which creak as if we were at sea.'

'Oh yes! It's wonderfully peaceful here, and most kind of you to have me.' The conte was much older than his sister, but remarkably attractive, Cecile decided. His waistcoat, of purple silk embroidered in gold, and the billowing sleeves of his shirt, like poured cream, would have made a dandy of him, but for the dark tunnel of his gaze.

Lucrezia had changed into a dress of scarlet hue, though her sash of emerald snakes was still about her waist. Cecile felt her own gown, in palest lilac, to be rather gauche.

'It's our delight to share our home with you.' Lucrezia passed Cecile butter for the warm bread rolls that accompanied their soup.

'My brother will think of nothing but birds while we're in

Italy, so I'm sure my time here will be more diverting.' Under the conte's penetrating eye, Cecile was gushing, saying what she would later find ridiculous.

'He took me once on a trip to the Norfolk flats, near Cley, to see the curlew sandpipers on their migratory path. It was horribly windy and threatening to rain, but Henry peered through field glasses for the longest time, passing them over now and then for me to admire some remote creature paddling through the reeds.'

Though Lucrezia proceded to dip her spoon to her soup, her lips were twitching. 'His wife, I am sure, can divert him to other pastimes.'

Lady Courcy cleared her throat, and the room fell quiet in contemplative mastication, before Lorenzo turned once more to his guest. 'The causeway is open for some hours each day, so you may venture into the village, though there is little there to amuse a young lady from London, I would think.'

'Please do call me Cecile. City life, while exciting in its way, is filled with multitudes of people. Here, I can breathe. I feel that something special is waiting for me—although the castle looked intimidating when I saw it from afar, like Bluebeard's fortress, or Thornfield, except surrounded by water, rather than forest, or moors.'

Lucrezia lowered her voice in a conspiratorial manner. 'And who is your Bluebeard? Who your Mr. Rochester?'

Seeing Cecile blush, Lady Courcy patted her hand. 'She's only teasing, my dear. Castles such as this make everyone feel that way, as if there are secrets in the walls. Real life is not generally made of the stuff of sensational novels, but I fear this place, perched between civilisation and the vastness of Neptune's empire, has history enough to fuel an entire library of sordid tales.'

Lorenzo's eyes had been upon his knife, the pad of his

thumb pressed lightly on the blade. He looked up; not at his aunt, but at Cecile. 'And would you wish to find danger here?'

'No... no! Of course not.' Cecile's tongue was suddenly clumsy in her mouth. She so wanted him to find her other than a simpering, silly girl.

The conte nodded for a little more Chianti to be poured into Cecile's glass, as a magnificent dish of hot spaghetti was brought to the table, steaming, and slippery with oil.

'May I say how much I admire your costume, Lady Cecile. The floral decoration at your neckline is most becoming.' Lorenzo made no pretence of hiding the direction of his stare, which rested upon the small swell of her bosom beneath her bodice trimmed with rosebuds.

'The flower is a symbol of awakening nature, of renewal, and youth,' remarked the conte. 'In Japan, the cherry trees blossom for just one week of the year, inspiring admiration not only for their flowers' beauty but for their very transience. In beholding them, we are reminded of the brevity of human life, of our own fragility.'

'How fascinating.' Cecile was glad for the change of subject. 'Have you travelled to the Orient?'

'I have.' Lorenzo's eyes captured those of his sister for a moment. 'Though the greatest mysteries, and joys, are often close at hand, rather than in places far abroad. The wisest among us appreciate what is right in front of them.'

His gaze moved from Lucrezia and fixed so intensely on Cecile that she was quite taken aback.

'My goodness, Cecile, you're feeling the full charm of my nephew this evening.' Lady Courcy lay down her fork. 'I hope you know enough of men to take such effusions with a pinch of salt—although it's true that you deserve the compliment.'

'*Brava*, Agatha,' declared Lucrezia. 'Cecile, I'm sure, is not so foolish as to believe every word of flattery.'

She shot Lorenzo a look of great smugness, but he continued, unabashed. 'My sister, as you see, is wearing scarlet: a colour which suits her well, representing the wilder aspects of her nature, and serving to warn the unwary. She is a work of human artifice, carefully cultivated in ways you cannot imagine, while you, Cecile, are truly nature's creation, pure and simple.'

'I'm sure you're too harsh upon Lucrezia,' asserted Cecile, though she startled herself with her forwardness. 'Meanwhile, I've no wish to be worshipped as anything other than I am.'

'How sensible you are.' Lucrezia gave her brother a sharp look. 'Men, I fear, are quite the opposite, wishing to be adored for what they believe themselves to be, rather than what they are—regardless of morals or prowess or intellect.'

'Now, children! No arguments, please. You'll spoil our enjoyment of Magdalena's cooking,' reprimanded Lady Courcy. 'Lorenzo, you must allow us to defend our sex and, in so doing, be somewhat hard upon yours.'

Lucrezia touched her wine glass against Agatha's, her eyes bright. 'You see, brother. You're outnumbered. We women are taught from birth to follow rules. To smile just enough, but not too much; to look a certain way, and behave a certain way. Really, you cannot be surprised that, on occasion, we rebel.'

'In that, dear sister, you seem to excel,' answered Lorenzo, retaining a tone of amusement rather than chagrin.

Cecile ventured another glance at the conte. *He's old enough to be my father, except that, I'm certain my own father was nothing like the conte.*

Before sleeping, she had, of late, let her thoughts wander to Lance, her Texan from the train. If she'd imagined anyone's arms about her, they were his. Now, she felt the stirring of something different: a feeling of dread and excitement as she looked at the conte's thin lips beneath his moustache, and the small, white, even teeth revealed in a half-smile.

She searched for some topic of conversation. Something to

say that would make him look at her again. Except that, she now saw, he *was* looking at her, without her having said a word, and her own eyes, which should have lowered in modesty, looked back at him.

'Although,' added Lucrezia. 'Now, I recall, on his last birthday, my brother dressed as Marie Antoinette, chest hair curling above his bodice. How was that, brother? Did it enlighten you to the disposition of women, to be corseted and struggling for every breath, as Society insists we must?'

'Indeed it did!' answered Lorenzo, swivelling his attention back to his sister. 'I wouldn't for all the world be born a woman, knowing the indignities to which your sex is subject.'

Lucrezia leant towards Cecile, speaking in a confiding whisper. 'His skirts were lifted more times than the French Queen's ever were.'

'Really, Lucrezia!' admonished Lady Courcy, whose hearing was still acute. 'Too crude!'

Cecile was most shocked, but found herself, nonetheless, suppressing nervous laughter.

'Not that I disapprove of people having their fun,' added Lady Courcy. 'The saddest part of aging is the setting aside of vices we no longer have the energy to pursue.' She sipped thoughtfully from her glass. 'These days, I content myself with novels.'

'Ah, the cheese!' Lucrezia clapped her hands as Violetta carricd in a large platter. 'The grapes are from the vines in our garden, Cecile. And we have *formaggio di capra* — cheese from goat's milk. You must try some.'

'Indeed you must,' agreed the conte. 'We use an ancient recipe, such as was enjoyed by my great-great grandfather, and probably long before that.'

'How long have your family lived here?' asked Cecile, accepting a slice to her plate.

'The castle was built in the thirteenth century. The original cannon remains upon the roof, directed out to sea, through the battlements.' His face took on a sudden sternness. 'However, I advise that you do not venture there, since I believe the roof is no longer sound, and the north tower staircase which leads to it is certainly dangerous. Several of the steps are crumbling. Better to avoid that part of the castello altogether.'

'No one uses that staircase.' Lucrezia, for once, seemed in agreement with her brother. 'Far too gloomy, and full of dust and cobwebs. Cecile shall admire the sea from the garden. No need to make herself dizzy on the roof.'

'Besides which,' the conte continued. 'There is the White Contessa, who walks the upper corridor by night, and climbs the tower.'

'A ghost?' Cecile ears pricked up. Here was a little of Otrano and Udolpho at last.

'There are many, but she is the only one who haunts that part of the house. You may hear her, perhaps, in the dead of night, sobbing for her lover. Her husband had him flayed before her, then hung his body from the window of the tower room, a rope about his neck, his flesh for the gulls to peck. It's said that the contessa cursed him, and all males of the di Cavour line, before slicing her own wrists. She was found the next morning.'

Oh! The horror! Cecile gave a strangled gasp.

Lucrezia dipped her finger into the camembert upon her plate. 'Every time he recounts the tale, the details become more obscene. It preys on his mind, of course, and I suppose we must all be allowed our little fantasies.'

'The di Cavour blood is strong,' answered Lorenzo, a small tick working in his temple. 'Dark, and furious, and sublime.'

'And not without a hint of madness,' added Lucrezia quietly.

'No doubt, extended bachelorhood produces an excessive

imagination, and a tendency to the morbid, Lorenzo,' chided Lady Courcy.

Lucrezia stared pointedly at her brother. 'Perhaps that is part of the curse. I don't believe the di Cavour men ever find true love, or true happiness. Isabella would enlighten us, I expect.'

'Least spoken on that subject is best,' suggested Lady Courcy. 'If Hell resides anywhere, it is in the recesses of the mind. Perhaps this is a curse all men suffer, to live under "mind-forged manacles", as Blake writes in his verse.'

The candles upon the table had sunk low, but there was flame enough for Lorenzo to ignite a cigar. 'Forgive me, ladies. Let us retire. Serpico shall walk with me in the gardens. The blooms are different by night, their scent more intense, more vivid. The night, we might say, brings a clarity impossible in the blaze of day.'

THE CORNERS of the room flickered in shadow but what light there was illuminated Lorenzo's face and he noted Cecile's blue eyes raised to him most prettily, her expression one of pleasing reverence.

Blonde wisps curled against the soft whiteness of her skin, and upon the slope of her exposed shoulder.

She is a canvas not merely unpainted, but newly stretched upon the frame. Perhaps, this conquest will offer more than amusement. Might she be worthy of bearing the next generation of di Cavours?

He recalled his father's skin, at the last, like the crust on cooling wax; his hands nobbled, age spots dappling the skin.

Those hands, shaking as they held a glass. The hands of a dying creature, near bloodless, nails ridged and horny. And his eyes, milk-clouded, caring no longer to see, nor his mind to remember.

In the dark hours, the cold fingers of mortality reached ever closer. Not yet, of course, but waiting.

Waiting.

CECILE STOOD AT HER WINDOW, listening to the sounds of the night: crickets, and the throb of toads above the rising tide, the far-off rush of the waves. Sometimes, she heard a distant wail, but it was only the rising wind, she told herself.

Moonbeams rippled across the olive grove, shivering the trees, and a tiny golden glimmer moved through the darkness. The glow of a cigar.

Past midnight, she succumbed to sleep. The house was still but for the scratching of mice, and the quarter-hour chime of the great clock.

Footsteps approached her door and the latch lifted, slowly, opening enough for fingertips to curl around the heavy oak. A face, pale, with eyes intent, looked long upon the sleeping figure.

8

BAD DREAMS TREMBLED beneath her lids.

'I'm here, my love.' Henry touched his lips to Maud's forehead and curled his arm about her waist. Still, her breaths came soft and gasping. Through the shutters, first light was creeping, but the villa was yet quiet.

A half-cry rose from her throat and she pushed her hands against his chest.

'Don't be frightened.' He pulled her closer. 'I won't leave you.'

She whimpered again.

Pushing down the coverlet, he caressed her breast, bending his head to take the nipple in his mouth, suckling. The tug of connection brought her twisting towards him.

The comfort was for her, but he grew rigid against her belly, wanting to slip into the ancient rhythm.

Even in sleep, she responded, her hipbone tipping to receive him.

'I love you, Maud. I love you.' Stroking her hair, he brought his hardness between her legs. As he entered, she gasped for air, surfacing from wherever she'd been.

He drove through all that separated them, buried inside. There was nowhere to go but within each other.

No more he and she.

MAUD WATCHED him pull on his costume for bathing, a towel over his shoulder.

'Join me.' Henry tugged her hand. 'Come and swim.'

Shaking her head, she remained at the dressing table. She misted the mirror with her breath. How quickly it lifted and vanished.

The room was as she remembered—the walls painted apple green, the bedspread patterned with oranges and lemons, and her musical box.

It still played. She'd wanted to be like the ballerina—dancing so beautifully, enchanting everyone. A gift from her father, his moustache tickling her cheek, smelling of pipe tobacco. Their game had been to place palms together, stretching her fingers to align with his. There had been solace in knowing that his would always be larger.

Someone is only dead when all who knew them are dead.

That's what people said.

Mountain climbing was a hazardous pursuit, and she'd been too little to go with them, her parents had insisted. The adventures would have to wait until she was fully grown.

She'd waited every day for months and months—until she'd accepted that they'd chosen the thrill of risk and peril over what they'd shared with her.

Was the desire to seek out danger in her blood?

Folding back the shutters, Maud sat on the window seat. Rancliffe had almost reached the cliff steps. She raised her hand to wave, although his head was turned away, and he was too far off to see.

Someone else was close by though; someone whose back and arms were strong, and whose skin was dark from the scorch of the sun. Someone with soil beneath his fingernails.

He looked up, and she beckoned.

9

THE CONTE, having consumed the last sliver of breakfast ham, dabbed his lips and set aside the tray. 'We should give our guest a tour of the castello, should we not?'

Sitting at his bedside, Lucrezia inclined her head. 'I hope you'll spare us from climbing every staircase. Cecile will better enjoy the sun and the open spaces of the garden.'

'We shall see. Too much sunshine is not good for the soul.' Pulling aside the covers, he approached the basin of hot water, made ready for his ablutions.

Before Lucrezia had time to leave he'd pulled off his night-shirt, presenting her with his bare buttocks. It was nothing she hadn't seen before but it annoyed her, nonetheless: this offhand treatment of any sensibility she might have.

'Don't leave on my account.' He soaked a flannel, passing it down his abdomen. Holding the cloth over his groin, he squeezed what lay beneath. 'The wager is as good as won. Let me claim my trophy now, and I may promise not to hurt you.'

His laugh followed her as she stalked to the door. Turning back, she spat at him. *'Maledetto! Vai all'inferno!'*

'Damn me to Hell all you like, sister-sweet. Just remember your bargain. When the time comes, you are to be a willing partner.'

Leaving Lady Courcy reclined on the terrace, they commenced in the library, the windows of which faced the open sea.

However, Cecile's eyes fell not, foremost, upon the books, but upon the carvings within the shelves. Each narrow section depicted creatures she recognized from mythology: the gorgon Medusa, and the multi-headed hydra, Cerberus guarding the gates of the next world, leaping satyrs and rearing centaurs— eyes ablaze, hooves and hands and necks twisting forward, as if to escape the confines of the wood. So many monsters and demons and angels, entwined in a Bacchanal, frozen in their macabre dance.

The ceiling, too, was intriguing: Cecile had never seen so much naked flesh, hands clutching, grasping, claiming. In the frescos of Florence's churches, and those of Rome and Venice, the faces of saints and sinners were contorted in similar states of agony and ecstasy. However, these were different; more violent, hungrier.

'The theme is Zeus' seductions,' explained Lucrezia, seeing Cecile's upward gaze. 'Leda with the swan, and Europa carried off by Zeus as a white bull. So predictable! Men always the ravishers and we the ravished!'

Cecile fought the flame in her cheeks. She knew her Greek mythology, of course—but she'd never thought of the stories in quite those terms.

Bringing her eyes back to where it was safer, she perused the spines ranged floor to ceiling.

She was familiar with her brother's many editions on birds, alongside works by the great poets and playwrights, and the ancient classics: Sophocles and Plato, Livy and Cicero. Here, the volumes were mostly Italian, though some were in English. But such peculiar topics: *The Extraction of Toxins from Botanicals*; *Madness: a study in hereditary affliction*; and *The Art of Trepanation*.

Trepanation? Wasn't that something to do with drilling holes to gain access to the brain? Were the di Cavours patrons of the healing arts?

With a shudder, she walked on. There would be some poetry perhaps. Tennyson or Browning, Rossetti or Arnold. She found them, at last, beside works by Manzoni and Carducci.

'*Goblin Market*, I think.' Lorenzo, standing only an arm's reach behind her, handed down a slim volume. 'Like pretty Laura, you have gold enough upon your head. Enough to purchase whatever your heart desires.'

He bent to lift a stray lock of her hair, as if to inhale the scent, but Cecile swiftly stepped to one side, tucking the errant curl behind her ear. His touch was not repellent to her; far from it. But, such familiarity went beyond what was seemly. Lady Courcy would not approve. She was not sure she approved herself.

Opening the cover, she made herself focus on the pages. 'Ms Rossetti's verse is beautiful. I won a prize, long ago, for its recitation, at the Beaulieu Academy for Ladies. The illustrations in this edition are enchanting.'

'They are by the great lady's brother, the infamous Dante Gabriel Rossetti. Such lips he draws, such eyes…' The conte's eyes, she couldn't help but notice, were upon her own lips.

'It will give me pleasure to think of it in your possession.' He gave a slight bow. 'It is yours.'

'You are too generous.' It was an expensive gift—but one

her brother would deem permissable for her to accept. She smiled shyly .'I thank you for it.'

Clutching the volume to her chest she walked on, stopping at a large, leather-bound edition which lay open upon the desk. It had long been pressed upon her that a lady did not raise her voice or express any extreme of emotion but, seeing the colour plate within, her exclamation burst forth unbidden.

Lucrezia moved to close the pages, glaring at her brother.

'Don't be a prude, Lucrezia.' Lorenzo sighed. 'Cecile is no schoolgirl. She may look if she wishes. My collection is at your disposal, Signorina.'

'That's... very kind.' She'd hardly had the chance to see what Lucrezia wished to conceal from her. Something else medical, perhaps? Her brief glimpse had shown a woman lying down— being examined, she supposed—and there were instruments on a table. What the doctor had been attempting, she couldn't say.

The conte's eyes followed where hers lingered—upon the closed cover. 'I judge no man, nor woman's, curiosity. Too many waste a lifetime justifying their own sins, while condemning those of others. An exhausting occupation.'

'Ignore him.' Lucrezia folded Cecile's hand over her arm. 'He takes delight in provocation.'

They came next to a long corridor, portraits spaced evenly along either side—an extended acreage of ancestors, faces stern and formidable.

'This is our father.' Lucrezia indicated a handsome man, the very image of Lorenzo, with the same air of disdain and pride. 'Don't be fooled by his good looks, Cecile. Our eyes are not always to be trusted in leading our heart on the wisest path.'

'Nor, always, our ears.' Lorenzo was standing so close behind Cecile that she felt his breath upon her neck. He touched her waist briefly, indicating they should continue onwards.

There was a series of the young Lorenzo: with his dogs, with his first horse, on Isabella's knee.

'And who's this?' Cecile stopped at another portrait, recessed into an alcove. 'Is it you Lucrezia?'

Her eyebrows arched. 'My father sent money to the orphanage in which I was raised, but he never visited me. Sons born far from the marriage bed may find a place, but rarely daughters. I doubt he had any image of me, not even a sketch in a forgotten drawer.'

'We should remedy that.' Lorenzo appeared again at their side. 'A reclining nude, I think. You have a figure worthy of immortalization, *mia sorella*, or so I would imagine...'

'*Diavolo!*' Lucrezia gave him a forceful pinch to the back of his hand.

'Have you any other siblings?' Cecile asked, thinking to divert the conversation.

'Probably, many.' Lorenzo shrugged. 'But I am the only legitimate heir.'

THEY ARRIVED next in the courtyard, entering a tiny chapel.

'How beautiful,' remarked Cecile. All about were marble saints, clasp-handed, and, above the altar, in stained-glass, Jesus stood in the desert. Tempted by Satan, his face was turned away in steadfast repose. 'It's remarkably tranquil. I suppose it must be the thickness of the walls.'

'Indeed,' said Lorenzo. 'There are many places in the castello where all is not as it seems. As in life, piety above and devilry below!'

Cecile didn't know what to make of Lorenzo's comment. Really, he said so many strange things.

Smiling at her puzzled expression, he moved to a heavy door, studded in iron, turning the key. It opened near silently, the hinges well-oiled for an ancient egress surely seldom used. He made a sweeping gesture. 'Follow me...'

A lantern sat nearby, and a box of long-stemmed matches. Lucrezia lit the wick. Steps spiralled down, taking them beneath the chapel, the flame casting a dull glow, swallowed by the darkness.

Even with her hem lifted, Cecile feared she might trip and tumble. The air had become still, subterranean dank, while the walls were damp to the touch. Her heels scraped stone, step by step, until they emerged into a space too large to be lit by the puny lamp. From somewhere beyond, there was a subdued, rushing sound, as of water moving.

The cold crept over Cecile, who wore no mantle over her flimsy gown.

'Our crypt.' Lorenzo's voice resonated. The lamp illuminated the hard edges of tombs.

Here, more than anywhere else in the castello, Cecile felt the breath of the past. Hewn from the same granite as the island it stood upon, the ancestral stronghold of the di Cavours had withstood centuries unchanged, holding captive the souls within until they found repose in the depths of its vault.

'We're almost level with the sea,' explained Lucrezia. 'The tide is coming in.'

There were other sounds: squeaks in the shadows, and the scratching scamper of small feet. Lorenzo raised the lantern, walking further, until the room narrowed, ending in solid wall.

The lamp brought to light iron hooks and tethers, leather straps and chains.

'And what do you think happened here, sweet Cecile?' Lifting her palm to the dank wall, he held it there with his own, his skin warm and dry, pressed to the back of her hand. She stood immobile, as if her limb were no longer part of her. And then, her hand was passed through cold metal, a circlet closing about her wrist. Her breath stopped with the heavy clunk of a bolt through the cuff's clasp.

'You are a captive of the crypt.' Lorenzo's fingertips brushed her collarbone, and she was suddenly aware of the uncertain space between fear and yearning. 'Scream, and none will hear you.'

For a moment, she saw nothing but his face, shadow-flung by the flickering flame, and the dark glitter of his eyes.

Would his single hand span my throat? What if he were to pull me close? Or to attempt a kiss? Would he dare?

Though she would never admit such thoughts, she had entertained them, reading Mr Stoker's book by candlelight, covers clutched to her chin: Dracula's visitation of Lucy, making her, night by night, his blood-bride, visiting her bedroom while mortals slept, to suck forth her soul. And, at last, transformed, his willing victim risen from her grave, beautiful in her undead state, driven by lusts no living woman might speak of.

Never before had those thoughts come to life so vividly in the presence of a man.

Lorenzo's voice was no more than a murmur, so that Cecile almost wondered if her own mind was conjuring the words.

'Can you hear them? Those who were manacled?' His breath was on her cheek.

'...stripped?' His lips brushed her ear. '...and beaten?'

'Really, brother!' Lucrezia's voice awakened Cecile from her strange reverie.

As if in his own trance, Lorenzo's eyes were half-closed.

Lucrezia freed the weight from Cecile's wrist, rubbing where the metal had left its mark. 'Poor Cecile will pack her bags and leave us!'

She led her back, past the mouldering remains of ancestors, and spiders scuttering, until they could see the staircase once more.

ON THE BAKED ROCKS, lizards sunned themselves, until the shadow of a bird caused them to dart for cover. It would have been too hot for comfort, but that the breeze played through the clifftop garden, lifting petals from their blossomed bowers.

Stretched out, legs bare, Maud peered at veined petals from below. Buzzing insects landed upon the fabric of her skirt, attracted by the bright colours of its floral sprig.

Beside her, Rancliffe had been sketching tiny finches and white wagtails, remarking on their gleaming plumage and jaunty tail feathers, recording, by means of his own onomatopoeic shorthand, their airborne melodies. Beneath their glorious top notes were the hums and clicks of Maud's realm of study.

Bathed in ruddy golden light, Maud had been observing the variety of life upon the trunks of olive and fig trees, and within the curtains of bougainvillea and jasmine. As in London, she noted where eggs were laid, and how emerging larvae chewed and wriggled.

She sought the ordering principles of trailing ants as they

worked together, using their feelers to pass messages as they foraged, and their collective strength to claim fallen fruit. With water-colour paints, she captured the iridescent shine of blue-backed beetles and the flaunted flare of caterpillars, blazed in yellow, lime and crimson.

She reached into the wells of lilies to pluck out flexing earwigs, and bent to look under the shading leaves of succulent aloe plants. There were a million unexplored places, and unnumbered creatures whose habits were unknown to her. How far did they act from instinct, and how far from intelligence, from learning: the termites designing their mound, and the wasps their nest, each with its intricate geometry. Not to mention the bees' endless obsession with the hexagon.

So many plants offered shelter, as if their residents had a hand in the almighty design, requesting the necessary corridors and chambers.

Drowsy with sunshine, Henry had long since put aside his notepad. He lay, long and lean, shirt-sleeves pushed up, his lightly-haired forearm shielding his eyes. Hearing Maud moving, he turned his head, watching her unfasten the small buttons of her blouse.

As their lips met, she guided him beneath her chemise.

Her nipple was soft under his fingers, then tight and hard, each squeeze sending the familiar, warm ache to her sex.

Bunching her skirts at her waist, his hand ran up the back of her thigh, stroking through the muslin of her bloomers, finding the delicate skin beneath the curve of her buttock.

She revelled in the constriction of his clothing, and hers, which must be overcome: buttons and fabric, layer by layer.

The world contracted to mouth and tongue, clench and thrust, limbs entwined and sweat-mingled, as if she were of his rib and, with relentless intent, wished to fuse again with her Adam.

IT WAS STRANGE, thought Cecile, that she saw so little of the conte during the day.

'He prefers the cool of his tower rooms,' explained Lucrezia. 'Or his library. The sun doesn't agree with him.'

Each evening, dishes arrived at the table, and Cecile surrendered to each delicious sensation: succulent crab and lobster, rich Ossobuco, served with risotto alla Milanese, ricotta-stuffed cannelloni, and zesty lemon gremolata. There were meringues and panna cotta topped with sweet raspberries, creamy zabaglione and tiny apricot pastries.

The conte asked about her London suitors. Shyly, she admitted there were none.

About her desire for children, she couldn't answer.

Did she ride, and hunt to hounds?

Had she ever suffered weakness of constitution, or serious illness?

Did she enjoy travel? Could she live in Italy, perhaps...?

'Have done with it and present Lady McCaulay with a ring,' exclaimed Agatha at last. 'Although it would be courteous to approach her brother before you enquire any further as to Cecile's readiness for marriage.'

Lucrezia drank more wine than was good for her, and blazed silently.

The mirror over the mantel in the dining room reflected the flicker of the chandelier; small points of light, quivering in that cavernous room, with its pomegranate-red walls.

Was Lorenzo Cecile's Hades, her forbidden temptation?

Her mind wandered, from the dining room, out, through the chill corridors, down to the damp, dark dungeon. She felt again the weight of a metal cuff about her wrist and cool hands touching where she longed to be touched. A face; impassive, imperious, close to hers.

CECILE CLOSED Mr. Stoker's book and replaced it on the night-stand. Her thoughts were not on the page, but deep beneath the castle, where the di Cavours lay in cold splendour. People once as alive as she, with all their hopes and desires, now still in their graves.

She ought to go to sleep but, as she reached to do so there was a creak beyond the door, then a gentle tap.

A spectre from the ancestral tomb?

The knock came again, louder.

'*Cara*,' whispered a soft voice.

Cecile watched as the latch lifted and the door inched open.

A white-gowned figure entered, hair dark about her face. 'You *are* awake!' Lucrezia tiptoed to the bed.

'Make room for me.' She wriggled beneath the embroidered quilt and her toes touched those of Cecile, making her start.

'How jumpy you are!' Smoothing the quilt, Lucrezia nudged closer. 'You remember, I promised to share my secrets…and, earlier, you thought the portrait in the long gallery might be me.'

Cecile gave Lucrezia an encouraging nod. The castle and its inhabitants had a strange fascination for her. She wished to know everything. 'If not you, was it your mother?'

'No, not her. Another, whose story is even more tragic.' Cecile's face displayed every bit of the curiosity Lucrezia had anticipated. 'A girl was born to the family before Lorenzo: Livia, older than him by two years. You recall the handkerchief you gave me? It was one she'd embroidered, with her own initial. And…' Lucrezia paused for effect. 'This was once her chamber.'

Cecile sat up in alarm. 'She slept here… in this bed?'

She drew back, as if the mysterious Livia might appear suddenly beside them. 'I hope she won't mind, wherever she is now, that I'm occupying her room.'

'She's in a place where I doubt she minds much about anything,' Lucrezia dropped her voice to a more confiding whisper. 'She became unwell—subject to fits of violence, her mind distracted.'

'How awful!'

'Awful, as you say, but some people are not born to happiness.'

'She was troubled from an early age?' asked Cecile.

Lucrezia lowered her eyes. 'Trouble visited her in the night, and she was unable to escape, until her own mind chose to escape through a tangled garden of madness.'

The hairs upon Cecile's arms prickled.

'She is a warning to us.' Lucrezia's voice was barely a murmur. 'That the act of love is not always sacred, and not always desirable. She was sent away—to an asylum, Lorenzo tells me. They discovered, soon after her arrival, that she was to have a baby.'

'Oh! But, but…She wasn't married!'

'Indeed not.'

'What happened?' Cecile's eyes were wide.

'When her time came, she lost the child, and her own death followed soon after. A blessing, we might say.'

The two fell into reflective silence, but Lucrezia glanced up through her lashes, to look at Cecile.

Such an innocent.

'We'd never wish to fall into trouble, would we?' asserted Lucrezia, her voice firmer now.

'Never,' agreed Cecile.

'Men see our virginity as a prize, and they wish to conquer it. So, we must resist.'

Cecile nodded. Even to Lucrezia, she dared not reveal the thoughts which came to her by night.

'Do you want to know what happens? When a man and woman lie together?' asked Lucrezia. 'I've been talking with Magdalena, and she's told me everything...'

'Really?' Cecile bit her lip.

'Oh, yes!' answered Lucrezia. 'And it's most shocking! Close your eyes, and I'll tell you, as best I can, of what happens to brides on their wedding night. Then, you shall know, and be prepared, and if a man who is not your husband attempts to seduce you, you shall be armed to rebuff him.'

Lucrezia's voice was soft as she related the journey of skin upon skin, and flesh within flesh, the words taking on a rhythm of their own.

No details were spared in Lucrezia's telling. Cecile felt the weight of the words, pushing and pressing upon her, as if their power would enter her body.

Cecile kept her eyes shut tight and, beneath the quilt, her hand crept low.

Then her dreams took her, and she tossed on her own inner sea.

She was a prisoner of the castle, steeped in the sea's salt-winded embrace, and her innocence the meal upon which her captor preyed.

A creature dark and threatening; a creature which scaled the sheer granite beneath her window. Like Lucy, in the book borrowed from Maud, Cecile felt the presence of her demonic visitor. She rose to welcome him and though she recoiled from the hunger in his eyes, there was no escape.

Laying her upon the bed, he crawled, hand over hand, peeling back the sheets. His nails were long and fingers slender —about her ankle, and then her shin, upwards, past her knee.

The beastly hand took every liberty with her body—finding her fur and stroking it until, like a cat relaxing under the caress of its master, her legs fell to either side, revealing her inner self to that creature's hand. And, all the while, there were those mocking eyes.

What power did Castello di Scogliera exert over her in those sleeping hours? From what place in her imagination did this creature emerge, to paw and seduce her body, to thrill and terrify her?

She heard it breathing.

Suddenly waking, Cecile remembered whose face it was that looked upon her, who saw beneath her skin. The face of one who slept within the castle walls.

CECILE LIT HER CANDLE. She might read again, but none of her books were likely to deter the dreams of which she was fearful.

Besides which, Lucrezia was asleep. To keep the wick burning would surely rouse her.

What then?

Cecile might venture to the kitchen, where jugs of fresh milk sat on the cool pantry shelf, alongside a possible remnant of Magdalena's peach tart.

Donning her dressing gown, she passed through the great hall, the clock chiming the half hour past midnight. The doors to the ballroom were flung wide, revealing its floor of gleaming black marble.

The room was still, but the echoes of the past seemed to call. She imagined herself in a gown of billowing purple, dancing across that dark-water surface.

Though she stood in shadow, as the clouds parted, the moon's pale crescent shone through the windows, illuminating the end of the room. The far door opened, and a tall figure entered, his hand clasped firmly about another's arm.

Cecile did not yet know the name of every maid in the castello. It was served by many silent feet and nimble hands, but Vittoria had the charge of Cecile's wardrobe. It was she who laundered and pressed the delicate muslins and silks worn by the elegant ladies of the household. It was she who heated water for Cecile's bath, and placed a warming pan in the bed.

Blowing out her candle, Cecile crouched at the edge of the doorframe. Though she understood little Italian, it was obvious to her that Vittoria was being admonished. The conte spoke with a hard edge not previously revealed in Cecile's presence.

The girl was sobbing. Imploring, struggling, she fell against a table. A vase toppled from its placement, smashing upon the floor.

Cecile leant forward, hardly caring now if she was seen. No servant should be disciplined by force, no matter their misdemeanour. Lorenzo's behaviour was unpardonable.

However, just as swiftly, the commotion ceased. Vittoria was not prostrate upon the floor, picking up pieces of broken glass. Instead, to Cecile's astonishment, Vittoria's face was upturned to her master. His hands clasped first about her waist, then moved lower, caressing her behind. Vittoria's arms reached brazenly around the conte's neck, drawing down his mouth to meet hers.

Cecile was unable to look away.

Whatever argument there had been was clearly mended, and whatever relationship existed between the two, it was far beyond her comprehension.

As she watched, the conte dropped to his knees, reaching beneath Vittoria's skirts.

He was drawing down her bloomers!

She was stepping out of them.

The conte brought forward a seat from the wall and then Vittoria did the strangest thing. She placed herself over his lap, face down, and remained quite still as he pulled up the layers of fabric—baring her legs, and then the orbs of her buttocks.

Raising his hand, the conte brought it down with unforeseen force upon one cheek.

Cecile's conscience insisted that she intervene. No one should endure such humiliation and ill-treatment. But, as a further smack reached its target, and another, Vittoria's cries spoke not of pain but of some other need, some desire which Cecile half recognized: beseeching not for punishment to end but for something else to begin.

The conte continued the ruthless dispatch of his hand and Vittoria's pleading grew fainter, as if in acceptance of whatever her master should choose to deliver upon her.

Cecile was transfixed, her mind telling her that she should depart—that the scene unfolding was not for her eyes. Her body, meanwhile, refused to obey.

All grew quiet again, but for Vittoria's soft moans. The conte's hand was no longer raised in savagery, but moved between the cheeks he'd so harshly assaulted, his voice murmuring in measured tones.

Lightheaded, Cecile resolved that she must return to her room; to remain would be unconscionable. Unsteadily, she rose from her crouching position, and cast one final glance at the dissolute scene.

The conte was no longer looking at the ample bottom provided for his amusement, but to the opposite end of the ballroom. To Cecile's dread dismay, he smiled.

How long had he known she was there?

'WHAT A SIGHT YOU ARE!' Lucrezia was sitting up in bed with a breakfast tray upon her lap. 'Have you not slept any winks?'

Cecile was too weary to appear cheerful.

'Something is bothering you, *cara.*' Pouring coffee from the pot, Lucrezia added cream and sugar, and handed the cup to Cecile.

Cecile so much wished to confide, but what could she say, and where would she begin?

'Tell me.' Lucrezia urged. 'I am your friend. I will help.'

Cecile sipped the coffee, drawing comfort from its sweet warmth.

'I woke from a… disturbing dream, and wanted to distract myself, so I came downstairs,' Cecile began. 'And then…I saw something.'

'Ah…' Lucrezia tapped her nail against the table.

At just that moment, there was a knock upon the door and Vittoria entered, carrying a second tray—of steaming eggs and slices of cured ham.

Cecile felt a sudden constriction in her throat.

As Vittoria looked up, Cecile was reminded of Maud—as she had seen her sometimes in the morning, wearing a look of serene satisfaction. Vittoria bore no look of shame, only slight surprise at being so scrutinized.

'*Scuzi.*' The girl bobbed her curtsey.

Lifting her cup again, Cecile found that her hands were shaking.

'Say nothing more. I know my brother, and his fondness for the young women in his service. Vittoria has not been so long with us. She is a novelty.' Lucrezia picked up some ham with her fingers. 'He is no worse than most men—very rarely to be trusted. We women must keep our wits about us.'

Cecile nodded mutely. One question preyed upon her mind.

Can I trust myself?

THE SUMMER HOUSE, Maud had written, the note left on his pillow.

The moon was dazzling bright, unsoftened by passing clouds.

Through the garden, Henry inhaled the night fragrance of lilies—ghost-white, smoke-sweet. Other feet had trodden there; other hands than his had brushed those blooms.

He heard them before reaching the final bend in the path. They were inside, but the doors had been left wide.

Maud sat upon the edge of a table, her skirts bunched on either side and feet raised to rest upon the sun-browned shoulders of the man kneeling. His hold upon her hips was firm, the taut muscles of his back contracting with each dip of his head.

At the ebbing of her final gasps, he turned, and Henry saw his wife's cream on Raphael's lips.

Reclining, her eyes half-closed, Maud looked at her husband and he looked back at her, at his Mademoiselle Noire. She spoke softly. 'We are born from the substance of this world, and we yield to it when we die. And, between, there is flesh and pleasure, and the thrill of every act that shows us how vividly we live.'

Henry knew what she wanted.

Raphael stood. Pulling the leather of his belt free, he let drop his trousers and kicked them away.

For what does our soul hunger, but beauty?

Raphael's was carved from daily labour, his abdomen hard, all the way down to silken curls, and the solid root of what made him a man. He stepped forward and there was a single touch. A soft meeting of lips. Then a rush of need.

Hands, rougher and stronger than Maud's could ever be, freed his thickness. He was hard in Raphael's palm, then hard in his mouth.

He was pushed to the floor. Raphael bore down upon him, belly to back. Teeth scraped Henry's shoulder. His arms were pinned.

Slick with sweat, they slid into one another, surrendering to the liquid dark.

1 4

CECILE HAD READ to the last stub of her candle when she heard the creak of floorboards outside her room.

'Lucrezia?' Cecile set aside her book. 'The door is unlocked.'

She rarely visited so late, but little about her was predictable.

'Lucrezia?' Cecile frowned. Usually, her friend barely bothered to knock before bounding into her bedchamber. Was it someone else then?

The hour was late for a servant to be called.

Before she had the chance to muse further, the footsteps walked on. A moment passed and they seemed to turn back—not walking but running.

Something must be amiss, for no maid would dare make haste in such a fashion unless there was an emergency.

Might Agatha have rung for assistance? Being so lively, one forgot her great age, and Cecile had been so wrapped up in herself, she'd hardly given thought to the welfare of Lady Courcy.

She must assure herself that the lady was well. Hurrying,

she pulled on her dressing gown, berating herself for letting the candle burn so low. She was but two paces from the door when the footsteps came again, running just as hard, then stopping abruptly.

There was a splintered laugh. Not that of Lucrezia; not like any laughter she'd heard before.

'Who's there?' Cecile's voice trembled.

In answer, there was a long scratch down the wood, as of a fingernail drawn slowly. As the latch began to rise, Cecile grasped it on her side. With her other hand, she slid the bolt. The latch rattled and there was a shuffling of feet; a woman's voice, muttering in Italian, then, hush.

Cecile rested her forehead against the door. Was someone attempting to unnerve her?

She should return to bed and ignore the attempt at intimidation. Nevertheless, part of her raged against doing so. She refused to slink under the covers like a frightened rabbit—and her concern remained for Lady Courcy. If she wished to resolve this, she ought to confront whoever was responsible.

She drew back the bolt and opened the door.

Immediately, the cool night-breath of the corridor slid past her cheek. The candle almost guttered, the little flame wobbling unsteadily, throwing shadows on the whitewashed wall. Beyond, the passage stretched into darkness.

No footstep. No laughter. No sound at all.

Lady Courcy's chamber was several along, past the bathroom they shared and a linen cupboard. Taking small steps, she inched forward. If a strange face were to rear up before her, she would scream, and rouse the household to her aid.

Reaching the third door, Cecile knocked lightly, then pushed it open. The room, shuttered against whatever moonlight there might be, was almost as dark as the corridor but she could make out the bed and Lady Courcy's sleeping form. She dropped the latch quietly behind her and, after brief hesitation, engaged the bolt.

The lady was resting peacefully, her mouth slightly open, emitting a gentle snore. Cecile wondered if she might slip under the covers on the other side. Certainly, Agatha wouldn't mind.

But, there was no reason for her to stay. It was her own nerves that made her uneasy to return to her room.

She must pull herself together.

She would impose on Agatha only so far as to take the taller candle from her stand. At least, then, Cecile could more easily navigate the passage.

Dipping the lit wick to light the other, she tiptoed to the door.

~

THE STEADIER FLAME of the new candle emboldened her.

Whoever had played their prank, there was no sign of them. All was quiet.

Cecile saw how foolish she'd been. No doubt, the castello was home to a host of servants she'd yet to encounter. Some might have been with the family for decades. Where masters were kind, elderly retainers were kept on regardless of slightly addled wits. The conte was clearly generous in this regard.

Lucrezia would know, and could ensure a more secure sleeping arrangement for the poor soul. However tolerant the household, one shouldn't be disturbed by those sort of night-time wanderings.

With that thought, the passageway presented no more fearful prospects. Cecile held the flame high and surveyed in both directions. Though the further ends remained indistinct, the candle provided a haven of light.

It was then that Cecile noticed the entranceway almost

opposite Lady Courcy's room: the door that led to the north tower. Unsafe, the conte had warned. Forbidden, for its crumbling stairs and hidden dangers.

A door usually locked, but now ajar.

Something impetuous quickened in her blood.

Why shouldn't she see for herself. If she were careful, keeping to where the tread was widest, it would surely be safe.

She climbed until, reaching the second curve in the upward spiral, she paused to catch her breath. The turret staircase was steeper than she'd anticipated and the stone walls seeped a damp sort of cold.

From above came a distant flapping sound.

Bats?

They roosted in high, abandoned places, didn't they?

Cecile envisioned them suddenly flapping all around her, tangling in her hair.

She spun about, wanting to scurry back the way she'd come but was arrested by the precipitous falling away of the steps. Lifting the hem of her nightgown, she made herself go carefully, feeling tentatively for each edge. She managed only four before stumbling, letting out a cry as her ankle gave way and the candle fell from her hand.

The darkness was immediate. Thick, oppressive, it bore down, pushing the air from her lungs. With the dark came a cloying muteness. Somewhere, water was dripping, but she couldn't have said whether those drops fell beside her or far above. Her ears were filled with rushing stillness and her own whimper.

And then a golden radiance was rising towards her, growing brighter. A low voice spoke her name and, from below, a man's face loomed, lit strangely by the flame before him; the face of the conte, his heavy-lidded eyes twin hollows.

The next moment, he was lifting her, hefting her hips against his shoulder, and they were descending, passing through the corridor, then over the threshold into her chamber. When he lowered her feet to the floor, she swayed—her head light and her ankle refusing to take her weight. She steadied herself against the arm encircling her waist.

He was holding her very close.

For a moment, she let him support her, too limp and shocked to protest. Only when his lips brushed her hair did her wits return. She had avoided seeing him all that day, much to her relief. Now, he was here, in her room. They were alone.

And all she could think of were the sounds Vittoria had made, bent over the conte's knee.

'You were looking for something, Lady McCaulay?' His tone was more seductive than disapproving.

'I apologize.' She realized she'd been holding her breath. Now, she let it out in a rush. 'Thank you—for finding me. I was imprudent in entering the tower.'

'Now, now. It is better to be honest. I see you are curious. It is only natural to be so when there is much you have yet to experience.'

She pushed lightly against his chest but he only nudged forward. To her surprise, her legs parted around his intruding knee.

'Let me go. I must lie down.' Her remonstration emerged barely above a whisper.

He smiled lazily. 'But, of course.'

Resting the candle upon the trunk at the foot of her bed, he promptly picked her up again, carrying her the short distance, hugged to his chest. The next moment, he had lain her upon her back across the coverlet and, to her horror, stretched out beside her.

She was aware of the hardness of his frame, presssed to her side.

With a twitch of his fingers, he loosened the ribbon which closed her dressing gown and pushed it aside, so that there was nothing between his hand and her body but the thin fabric of her nightdress.

'Sir, I beg you. This is not gallant.'

His eyes held hers as his palm settled upon her breast, stroking through the flimsy muslin. A groan escaped his throat. '*Mia amore.* I am at your mercy.'

She twisted away, but as his teeth grazed her neck, molten pleasure welled inside her.

'It is no sin to desire. Struggle if you wish, but I see your passion. Your every look betrays you.' His mouth followed where his fingers had touched, and he was moving above her, shifting his weight. His hand caressed her side, drawing up her nightgown.

'No!' She grasped her hem as it reached her thigh. Her body responded to his touch and her heart raced, but her instinct rebelled against such base behaviour.

'We are not... I can't!' With all her strength she rolled him from her and was surprised to find that he let her do so.

Quickly, she knelt up, then scrambled from the bed, doing her best to ignore the jarring pain in her ankle. Pulling her robe closed, she spoke as forcefully as she was able. 'You forget yourself, Sir.'

He made no further move to assault her, but his expression of remorse seemed a little overplayed. 'See how you heat my blood, sweet one. A man's ardor is apt to run away with him. Even a little encouragement is our undoing.'

Cecile pursed her lips. She was certain of having done nothing to provoke such an invasion of her person. Then again, what did she know of men? What did she know of the conte? That he was a womanizer, and not to be trusted—as Lucrezia had warned.

At least, he had been gentlemanly enough to cease his attentions. She would have been obliged to scream other-wise, and how much worse that would have been. She knew how gossip travelled. Such things rarely remained secret.

The situation was highly compromising. If Henry found out…

No, that mustn't be. I won't allow it.

Raising her chin, Cecile did her best to assert her dignity. 'If you have any care for me, I beg you will say nothing of this… misunderstanding.'

He sat up, straightening the cuffs and cravat of his evening attire. 'A misunderstanding, yes—and our secret. I understand.'

She disliked the idea of being drawn into a "secret" but it was too late to quibble over what they might call the thing. She needed to affirm her position as a woman of reputation and virtue. 'I trust to your honour, conte. What happened, or almost happened…'

His lips twitched, as if enjoying her discomfort.

He levelled his gaze, but not quite to her eyes. She felt his stare upon her body, as if he were looking through her clothing to the flesh beneath.

She pulled the sash of her dressing gown tighter. 'I was disoriented from my mishap in the tower. I would never…' She cleared her throat. 'Intimacy of that sort is rightfully reserved for wedlock.'

'Wedlock, yes.' Rising from the bed, a single stride brought him before her and he took her hand, lifting her fingers to his lips. 'It is somewhat forward of you, but I appreciate your desire for propriety. You wish us to be married before giving yourself with full fervour.'

'That really wasn't…' Exasperation swept over her. He had an infuriating habit of distorting even the simplest sentiment. 'That is to say, I would never presume…'

'Say nothing more, *mia amore*.' Turning her wrist, he lowered a kiss to where her pulse flickered. 'Doubt not that I shall revisit the memory of our sweet rendezvous and, with every beat of my heart I shall be yearning for the hour in which we may be better acquainted.'

With that, he bowed and exited the room, closing the door gently behind him.

Dear God! Cecile found that her legs could no longer support her.

Staggering to the bed, she buried her face against her pillow.

What had just happened?

Did he truly harbour feelings for her? Was it possible? She had been his guest little more than a week.

And what had possessed her to allow him such freedoms? She had thought herself chaste, but she hadn't struggled—at least, not at first.

To what would she have submitted, had she not come to her senses?

Her mind skittered away from the answer; yet her body knew.

THE NEXT MORNING, Cecile's ankle ached a little, but finding she could walk upon it, she resolved not to make a fuss. The last thing she wanted was to explain how she'd come by the injury. She would simply pretend a little tiredness, take a longer than usual afternoon nap, and attempt to stay off her feet.

Most of the night, she'd lain awake, attempting to decipher her feelings. Cecile hardly trusted her recollection, but the conte had given a strong impression of wishing to ask for her hand. Could it be that she'd ignited a true devotion?

He was eligible and titled—all the things Henry would desire for a match. A great deal older than her, of course, but such things were not generally considered an impediment.

It would not be unpleasant to call myself a countess, and be mistress of this garden and the castle. A man mellows under the influence of a wife, so they say. I would be the mother of his children, his contessa, his lifetime companion... and I would have position, and wealth.

Lucrezia would be always with me. What wonders we might

discover together, all the world at our feet.

And, once wed, would Lorenzo not give up his flirtations?

Surely, I would be enough, as his bride...

The conte would touch her as he had done last night; his hands reaching to possess her, his mouth claiming ownership of her skin, his eyes penetrating her very soul.

She thrilled to imagine it.

Yet, her heart told her to be wary. She had witnessed for herself the conte's dissolute ways, and Lucrezia had warned against trusting her half-brother.

Everything was so confusing, and Cecile had so little experience to draw upon. She might confide in Lucrezia, but her intuition told her that her friend would not be pleased. From the first, she had seemed set upon making Cecile aware of the conte's shortcomings.

She needed more time—to reflect on her own state of mind, and to learn more of the man who wished to become her suitor. Except, perhaps, it might be useful to hear Lady Courcy's opinion on the matter.

Knocking on Agatha's door, she found her sitting at her dressing table, brushing out her silver hair.

'Does Isabella still dye hers that improbable shade of blue?' Agatha plaited the length before coiling it in place.

'At Maud and Henry's wedding, it was lilac,' answered Cecile. 'It suited her.'

'Of course, my dear.' Agatha pinched her cheek. 'What a kind girl you are. Now, come and sit with me.'

Moving to the chaise, Agatha stroked the faded green brocade. 'I remember sitting on this seat, years ago, when Isabella was newly married and I came from London, to visit. The two of us met during our year of coming out, and I was soon introduced to her older brother. We danced and chatted at the various balls and soirées but only at Isabella's wedding did we fall in love. How could we not, in such a place as this, under the Mediterranean sun?'

Cecile sighed wistfully. It was the sort of romance she'd dreamt of for herself.

'We can have anything our heart desires. The tricky thing is determining what that is exactly. Are you having trouble deciding, Cecile?'

She didn't trust herself to speak, but Agatha seemed to sense, at least in part, her anxieties.

'I knew Lorenzo's father well. What poor Isabella endured! He was a reprobate and a gambler, and a seducer of women. Look at our young Lucrezia, born of his affair with that Milanese singer.' Agatha gave a sniff of disapproval. 'Talented she may have been, but no good sense at all, abandoning her baby and throwing herself from the roof of the opera house! It's the stuff of those Penny Dreadfuls!'

Cecile wondered, faced with the same situation, how she would behave. The thought of such a thing brought a terrible constriction to her throat.

'The old conte paid to house Lucrezia in a place for… unwanted children, and she was conveniently kept away from Polite Society,' continued Agatha.

Cecile shifted in her seat, uncomfortable in discussing the details of Lucrezia's upbringing—though she knew her new friend would care not a jot. It was one of the things Cecile most admired about Lucrezia: that she rose above the commonplace need for approbation.

'I must warn you,' Agatha went on, 'Lorenzo has followed the same path of riotousness as his father before him. He's charming, of course, when he chooses to be. Enough women have fallen at his feet. Some even fool themselves into thinking him besotted.'

Cecile picked at the embroidery on a cushion.

'Still, we must give credit where it's due,' conceded Agatha. 'Lorenzo took up Lucrezia's guardianship on his father's death, and has kept her close ever since. She's become quite a lady. One would never guess...'

She gave Cecile's hand an affectionate squeeze. 'It's best to know something of the world, my dear, and navigate it wisely. Young women are too often brought up with their heads in the clouds.'

'Are all men like that—taking what they want without care for the consequences?' asked Cecile.

Lady Courcy hesitated to answer. 'Not all. Maud tells me that Henry worships her. A genuine love match, it seems.'

'It's true that Maud understands him—better than me, I sometimes think.' Cecile remembered her many hours alone on their travels through Europe.

Whereas I barely understand myself.

'The sun is going to be especially hot today.' Lady Courcy added some more hot water to her breakfast teapot. 'I shall stay inside, where it's cool—and you may find me if you need me.'

From her tray, she selected a slice of buttered toast. 'I'm so very pleased that you and Lucrezia are becoming friends. You'll be a good influence on her. She is wild at times, but your steady nature will set her the appropriate example.'

Agatha fluttered her fingers in dismissal. 'Only remember to wear your hat, my dear, and keep to the shade where you can. An excess of heat can make one feel most peculiar.'

Lucrezia had set out a picnic on the second terrace.

'How wise we were to abandon our corsets. Now, we may eat as many pancakes as we like, warm from the griddle, with nothing to hinder us!' She passed the honey, having poured some liberally onto her plate.

In the bold sunshine, the events of the night seemed but phantasms. Nevertheless, Cecile felt compelled to ask Lucrezia if she'd heard anyone roaming in the night, or knew who might have been scratching at her door.

'Ah yes.' Lucrezia spooned the last of the fig compote from the jar, directly into her mouth. 'There is nothing to worry over, my Cecile. I know well of whom you speak—someone who has been here a long time, as you speculate, and who is under my brother's protection. She walks in her sleep and is apt to strange behaviour. He shall see that this person is kept more safely in her bed.'

She narrowed her eyes. 'Still, keep your latch bolted. Doors are best locked in this castle anyway. My brother is fond of the company of young women, and the temptation of your unsecured door may be too much for him. Do not allow yourself to become his plaything, Cecile. Remember, if you will, the fate of my mother. Remember, poor Livia...'

Cecile took up a peach, and a knife to peel it with. 'I know it's foolish to fall in love too easily.'

'You're not in love at all, I should hope.' Lucrezia looked quite stern.

'People marry for other reasons than love, don't they? Besides which, if I were to marry him, you and I would truly be sisters, together always.'

'It would be a high price to pay.' Lucrezia placed her hands upon Cecile's shoulders. 'Be careful, for you are looking into the twilight, and in pursuing my brother, you would have not the faithful dog, but the greediest of wolves.'

'Agatha said much the same.' Cecile worried at her lip. 'As my chaperone, she's keeping her eye on me, as Henry told her to, I suppose.'

'She's a funny bird, I think you say.' Lucrezia rose, beckoning Cecile to follow. They stood where the terrace fell away, admiring the unhindered view of the sea beyond.

The warm breeze lifted the delicate fabric of their dresses, making them billow behind. Despite her ankle, Cecile felt the strength of her body, standing in resistance to the moving air. How marvellous it was to have only the muslin against her skin, and to relax into the natural rhythm of breathing, without the constriction of whalebone stays.

Lucrezia squeezed her elbow. 'Have you seen her photographs? All of the dead people of her youth: writers, artists and musicians. I wonder, sometimes, if any were her lovers.'

'Lucrezia!' admonished Cecile. 'Even if you think such things, you shouldn't say them.'

'Nonsense. I see Agatha, as Flaubert says, her 'dry bones quivering with joy' at the remembrance of passion past. At least, I hope it is so. How sad it would be to reach such an age and have no memories to call upon.'

'Well, perhaps...' conceded Cecile. 'But there must be more to look back on than love affairs. There are all sorts of things I want to do, besides...' she was unsure quite how to conclude her sentence.

'In this, we agree, *mia piccola.*' Lucrezia took Cecile's hand. 'We shall make our own happiness, without relying upon any man.'

FROM HIS TOWER, Lorenzo looked down upon them: Lucrezia's arm slipping about Cecile's waist and their heads, dark and fair, held close. The breeze moulded the flimsy fabric of their dresses to slender curves. He lingered upon the image; the swell of breasts, and legs parted to the teasing wind.

IT WAS past midnight again when Cecile woke, her pulse quickened. Pulling back the shutters, she threw open her window.
Far below, the waves churned and a night-bird flapped past
with a baleful screech.

In her dream, she'd imagined herself a bride in white silk,
wearing a tiara of pearls. The ring had been upon her finger
and she the mistress of the castle. Except that her groom had
not led her to the comforts of his bed but straight from the
chapel down the dank steps, to the obscurity of the crypt.

His clasp upon her wrist had been firm, dragging her to the
manacles, in the deepest shadows of that foul place. 'And, now,
my contessa,' the voice had said, both seductive and cruel.
'How shall we spend our wedding night?'

Strong hands had rent the bridal gown, until her pale body
quivered before him and her arms, outstretched, ached from
the constraint of their imprisonment.

She closed her eyes against the memory. What caused her
to think such things? Never before had dreams like these

plagued her; only since coming to this place—only since meeting *him*.

Unlocking her door, she peered down the passageway, considering descending. The freshness of the garden would revive her.

Why then did she make her way towards where Lorenzo's apartments were located, to his solitary tower?

One foot in front of the other, she climbed until reaching a door left ajar.

His bedchamber.

Would she find him asleep, or as wakeful as she?

And what impulse brought her there, to the threshold from which there would be no return?

She stood for some moments, waiting for him to see her candlelight and invite her entry, but all was silent.

Extending her arm, she pushed open the door.

The room was well-furnished: the floor covered in fine rugs, the curtains swagged in rich velvet. And, there was a bed.

His bed.

A bed that rose high from the ground, its canopy hung with golden brocade.

But there was no head upon the pillow, despite the late hour.

Cecile looked back the way she'd come. What if he were to appear now, and find her? A shiver overtook her; fear, and something else...

She ought to return to her own room. Instead, she allowed her feet to lead her upwards, through another two rotations of the curving stair.

There was another door; another room—this time, locked.

There were voices. Coming from above—or from the other side of the door?

She rested her ear to its wood, hearing nothing but the far-off murmuring of the sea.

A chill draught had descended. A window, somewhere, must have been left open—yet, at that moment, the castle appeared a living thing, the air drawn through its passages like breath. Flinching back, she collided with the cold stone of the wall behind.

What was she doing?

Hurrying away, she drew level again with the conte's bedchamber—and something tugged inside her chest.

Would the key to the other door be in his room?

Madness possessed her. Entering once more, she set her candle upon the nightstand. She opened the drawer; nothing but papers. On top was a small box; only cigars.

Where else to look?

There were several wardrobes, filled with suits and hats, drawers of gloves and cravats. She couldn't possibly search them all. Time was passing.

And then she saw it.

A key upon a ribbon, hanging in plain sight, from the centre of the canopy above the bed.

It took but a moment and she had climbed up, her fingers reaching.

CECILE OPENED the door only a little; enough to admit her entry, closing it immediately behind. By the flicker of her flame, she discerned a corner chest, a chair, horse tack and riding switches on the wall. The room was being used for storage, perhaps.

How peculiar for such a place to be locked. There's nothing here of interest.

To one side several wooden objects lay upon a table—most bulbous at one end, sometimes both. Some were curved, others straight. She picked one up. Smooth, polished, and quite heavy.

Walnut wood? It sat well in her palm. Her fingers closed about it.

The conte is well-travelled. Tribal items from Africa, or totems?

She'd read of such things.

Suddenly weary, she sunk upon the chair. Heavily padded and upholstered in dark velvet, it was surprisingly comfortable, but unusual in shape—with slender, gilded arms, protruding upwards.

For invalids, that they might grasp these and pull themselves upright?

There was a little platform beneath, perhaps to aid in mounting the chair.

Like climbing upon one's horse, Cecile decided, endeavouring to understand the design.

She had a vague memory of having seen something similar, though she couldn't recall where.

There was something else, behind the door. A strange contraption, with cogs and wheels. Turning its handle, a chain link moved noisily. A most peculiar device, and she couldn't begin to imagine what use it served. Perhaps no use at all, since it had been relegated to this out-of-the-way location.

What had she expected to find?

It was all rather disappointing.

At the far end of the room was a picture.

Some out-of-favour relative, banished to this forgotten storeroom?

As she drew close, she saw that it was no di Cavour depicted, but a woman from the Orient.

A souvenir from the Far East, of course, where Lorenzo has travelled.

Cecile raised her candle. The background was filled with Oriental script, and the lady's face was upturned, a little octopus sitting beside her ear. Cecile was used to seeing dogs and horses in paintings, birds and cats, on occasion—but never an octopus.

It's whispering something to her. How fascinating are the Chinese; or is this Japanese?

She moved the candle across, and her hand began to shake. For the lady was quite naked, and there was a delicate tentacle wrapped about her nipple. Another, thicker, encompassed her thigh. Several curled around her arms. One draped possessively across her stomach. Between her open legs was the head of a terrifyingly huge octopus, its beak lowered, as if to devour her. And yet the woman appeared not to struggle, or be in distress.

Cecile couldn't help but look, and look again. So many tentacles. Caressing and engulfing.

Her eyes returned to the horse tack, except that she realized, now, it was no such thing. This metal and leather was never intended to bridle a mare, and while several of the switches were, undoubtedly, horse whips, some were not. Their handles were too short, and their tails too long and thick, stained crimson-dark.

She looked again at the chair and at the mangle, and recalled her brief glimpse at the book in the library. Figures half-clothed, contorted awkwardly.

There was something here she didn't comprehend, yet her imagination placed her over the end of the chair, bending, the conte raising her gown with the tip of a switch, her face burning with shame as his hand found her bare flesh.

'I FEAR you must prepare yourself, my dear, for my winning of our little bet.'

Lorenzo sat before the dying embers of the fire in his private sitting room, cigar in hand. Lucrezia, in her dressing gown, her long hair plaited for sleep, warmed her back to what heat remained. It had begun raining, and the night had grown unseasonably chill.

'Her terror at the prospective assault on her virginal state offers more entertainment than I'd foreseen!' he observed. 'She positively pants to be seduced, while tormenting herself with her own wickedness.'

'Don't be so sure of your victory. She will submit to my kisses as easily as yours, taking my embraces as sisterly affection before realizing to what she commits herself and, then, in the heat of the oven, will rise to me as sweetly as new-baked bread.'

'She may require a coarser hand than yours to lead her astray,' Lorenzo countered. 'One inclined to force, rather than teasing pleasure. How deliciously she would struggle at being punished over my knee, and how rapturously she would beg for more. The anticipation of it is most diverting.'

Lucrezia rolled her eyes. 'You are nothing if not predictable, brother. Meanwhile, if you wish to play your games with Vittoria, it would be prudent to do so behind a locked door. Cecile no doubt thrilled to her unexpected act of voyeurism, but you may frighten her off altogether if she thinks you too engrossed in our servants' charms.'

'Perhaps I wish to begin as I mean to go on,' answered Lorenzo. 'Let her see that she must compete for my affections. In point of fact, I rather fancy she would put up with a great deal, if the enticement were sufficient. As the next countess, I believe she would do very well, and endure whatever dalliances I pursued as those due to a hot-blooded nobleman of the di Cavour line.'

His attitude gave Lucrezia pause. Once he truly set his mind to the acquisition of a prize, he was relentless.

'She might be persuaded into all manner of sport, once the family diamonds are at her disposal.' Lorenzo puffed thoughtfully on his cigar. 'From what we saw in the crypt, she appears particularly disposed to being restrained, which makes things a great deal easier. It's always interesting to see how far a "lady" will surrender herself when she feels her own will is no longer an obstacle. All the trappings of defiant struggle may be observed, while the body submits to the true spirit of debauchery.'

For all her exasperation with Cecile's naïvety, Lucrezia could not help but pity her. To marry Lorenzo would be a harsher sentence than she would wish upon any woman. Far better for the coddled innocent to succumb to Lucrezia's embraces, and escape with her liberty.

She knew Lorenzo's darker inclinations, and that her own avoidance of submission could not be indefinitely extended. Lucrezia would need to find another path, away from his guardianship, and the power he held over her.

'My inclination is to marry her without further ado.' Stretching out his legs, Lorenzo exhaled smoke plumes. 'Lacking the patience for a prolonged courtship, I might take my prize, and sire the next di Cavour heir in one swoop. It would be a pretty piece of work for one evening, would it not?'

Lucrezia turned away, refusing to be goaded.

'No doubt, Lady McCaulay will positively run to the altar once her maidenhood has been lost. I might even allow her to believe herself in love.'

'You're too kind, I'm sure.' Lucrezia clenched her fists. If she but knew for certain that provision existed for herself in Lorenzo's will, she would swiftly arrange his demise. His machinations, and his tastes, had long been repugnant to her, and the leash was tightening upon her neck with each day that passed.

'Of course, no wife should bask too long in the uncondi- tional love of her husband.' Lorenzo approached the hearth, tapping out the ash from his cigar. 'True devotion is best inspired by a desire to please, isn't it, my dear.'

Standing close, he wrapped the length of Lucrezia's dark plait around his fist and pulled, so that her neck bent back. 'Naturally, there will still be a place for you.'

He touched her exposed throat. 'There are plenty of ways in which you may be party to the merrymaking, sister dearest. And, Serpico, you know, is very fond of you. Such a faithful servant, and deserving of sharing in the same pleasures enjoyed by his master.'

Pushing aside the yoke of Lucrezia's night attire, he exposed her collarbone. It was his mouth she expected to descend there but, instead, she felt a sudden heat. He tugged down the fabric further, his fingers hovering above her breast, holding close the glowing tip of his cigar. With a cry of fear, she jerked back but his grip upon her hair was firm.

'I've plans enough for you, when the hour comes. But, in the meantime, we may taste a little of your fine wine. It's a simple matter to uncork the bottle.'

He threw the stub into the fire and moved to unbutton his breeches but Lucrezia punched him abruptly where her blow would have most effect. As he doubled over, she twisted about, unhooking his hold upon her plait, contorting his arm behind his back.

'You may find I have a bitter aftertaste.' Hissing, she pressed his head to the hard marble of the mantle. He swore, gasping as she wrenched his arm higher.

'You enjoy pain, do you not, brother?' Taking the side of his hand between her jaws, she bit down hard.

He swore again but Lucrezia's elbow in the small of his back brought him to his knees.

With his blood in her mouth, she stalked away.

HAVING LOCKED the door of the fearful room, Cecile hurried back to the conte's bedchamber. The mattress creaked under her feet as she replaced the ribbon, threatening to topple her.

Looking down at Lorenzo's bed, she pictured her own head on the pillow, and he above, his body pressing heavily. Weak-legged, she descended.

If she were discovered by him, in her intrusion…

She moved swiftly, her footsteps light upon the wooden floor of the passageway, darting to avoid the places where she knew it squeaked. She reached her door, but her heart was hammering so rapidly.

She needed to calm herself. A tonic, or a strong drink. Wasn't that what was recommended?

Henry had never permitted her to take spirits. A little wine, or a glass of sherry, only. In the library, there were decanters. Brandy, perhaps. Doctors gave it to calm the nerves.

The clock chimed one as she took the main stairs downward and crossed the hall, lit by pale moonlight through tall windows.

Passing the shelves of books, she moved directly to the table upon which the crystal decanters were kept, unstoppered the first and sniffed. The liquid was pungent, reminding her of smoking bonfires and aniseed. She poured a little into a glass and raised it to her lips. It burned, and made her splutter, but the warmth was quickly inside her. There was comfort in it, despite the vile taste.

A little more, and she would be calmed enough to return to her bed.

With the glass emptied, she rubbed at the rim with her nightdress and replaced it upon the tray.

Her pulse was steadier now and her eyes roamed upwards —to the ceiling, where fleeing women ran, mouths agape in terror and in warning, pursued by the beasts of Zeus' seductions.

She paused to look upon the ancient volumes, touching the old leather.

One was embossed with a golden serpent, coiled through the spine. Its small, bronze clasp opened easily, loose on its hinges. *Efficacious and Undetectable Poisons.*

The book was dirty, inside and out, with the grease of many fingers. It fell open at "Ridding the Body of Unwanted Pregnancy". The ink was smudged, as if from something spilled.

Cecile snapped it closed. She had no desire to think on such things.

The monsters of ancient mythology, carved into the shelves, looked down on her, eyes sharp and mouths sneering. The whole room, she might imagine, was mocking her. She did not belong there. There were secrets in these books, as well as within these ancient walls, and the castle's many rooms; they were best left undisturbed.

As she turned to leave, there was a shift in the shadows.

Someone was approaching, carrying their own small source of light.

There was just time for Cecile to blow out her candle, and hide behind the curtains.

With a firm footstep, the person crossed the room, striking a match to ignite the oil lamp upon the desk.

She heard pouring from the decanter and a grunt of satisfaction. The tumbler was refilled and knocked back once more; and a third time, the glass landing heavily.

'*Cagna di coraggio. La farò pagare!*'

Cecile had no need to peek from her hiding place and no desire to do so. She knew that cursing voice. The thought of Lorenzo discovering her twisted a coil in her stomach.

Only when he'd left did she creep out. The decanter was almost drained.

The lamp's flame remained lit and, in its pool of light, Cecile saw the glass, the very one from which she'd drunk. Bloody fingerprints were upon it. Something dark had dripped across the rug.

It was not only the gentleman on the pale horse who came for us in our bed in the ripeness of old age. The villainous might lend a hand, delivering souls into the rider's embrace. Poison, blade or the quiet dispatch of the pillow on a sleeping face: the tools of those doing amateur business for the Reaper.

She knew violence existed beyond the flights of fancy in her novels, and that poison lurked in human veins, as potent as any administered into a pie-crust or pot of tea.

With shaking hand, she lifted the lamp, and made her way back, through the darkness.

18

Nature was remorseless, random, brutal and beautiful; logical and yet unfathomable. If Maud studied the ants and bees and beetle-life, each with its own purity of design, would she find clues to a hidden purpose in her own life?

She stood at the top of the villa's spiral staircase, looking down through its curving descent. It made her think of the theories of Mr Gaudi and the power of the cosmos—the movements of which combined with gravity to generate the spiral motion of water, from the swirling stir of the greatest oceans to the propensity of her bathwater to funnel down a plughole.

The same inward, spiralling movements were found in the animal and vegetable kingdoms, from the snail's shell to the falling motion of a winged sycamore seed.

And what of me?

She stroked the as yet imperceptible swell of her stomach.

Am I spiralling in ever smaller circles?

Despite all her efforts to forge her own path, was this how it ended?

'The other world is calling you.' Maud's voice was a whisper. 'Part soil and part starlight, we exist between the Earth and Heavens.' She tied a sash about Rancliffe's eyes, and another bound his hands behind.

As she retreated with a swish of skirts, he was reminded of another time, long ago it seemed, when she'd passed behind her seated audience, and he'd sought the touch of her gloved hand.

Against his bare back, the olive tree's bark was rough. Alone, exposed, he shivered, despite the lingering warmth of the fading sun. Through air thick with sea-salted-brine came the buzz of cicadas. A nightjar added its low, churring call.

There were footsteps on the path; female voices—hushed, speaking rapidly in Italian. How many, he couldn't tell, but Maud's was not among them.

'*Guarda!*'

'*Lui è bello.*'

Drawing close, they brought with them the scent of their bodies. A tentative hand touched his naked chest, brushing his nipple.

With understanding, his heart beat faster.

Fingers fluttered across his abdomen, tickling downward into the thatch of his pubic hair. As a hand grasped the root of his cock, Rancliffe's breath caught.

Stroking, the woman whispered encouragement. '*Crescere per me...*'

Her breathing was as rapid as his own. She stood closer, her skirts either side of his knee, leaning in.

A hand settled upon his buttock, giving a gentle squeeze. '*Buona e ferma...*'

The women giggled again, but quietened as they saw that

he'd been brought to full prominence. There was a note of urgency in the exchanges that followed.

'*Devo essere il primo!*'

'*E io dopo.*'

He recognized those phrases well enough. They were arguing over who would have him first, but the dispute ceased as a mouth lowered, tongue and soft inner cheeks caressing; sucking his length, releasing and taking him again.

'*È delizioso,*' murmured she who enveloped him, humming with pleasure.

He moaned.

'*Lo voglio.*' Skirts lifted and he felt the press of a straddling leg: fur and heated moisture. She rubbed her sex upon his thigh.

'*Il mio bel uomo inglese.*' The woman sighed, and her lips closed upon his nipple.

A willing slave to fingers and insistent mouths, he soon groaned his release.

They lay him down then, untying his hands briefly—only to secure them above his head.

Bringing him to fullness again, they took turns bestride him, drawing him inside, clenching his girth—and all the while exclaiming to one another.

He was their toy; their aristocratic Englishman, with his hair the colour of scorched summer meadows. Nothing like their husbands.

Rancliffe was lost, his cock achingly hard, his skin warmed by silken touches and cooled by the twilight.

Unseeing, he submitted, his body their plaything.

THE NIGHT IS MADE from stars, as much as from darkness.

They looked down, eyes aglitter, watching as Maud watched, and someone else too.

There was another pair of eyes, unseen. The eyes of one who would report to his master.

19

'IT IS NOTHING, I'M SURE,' answered Lucrezia, to Cecile's impassioned outpouring. 'My brother is many things, but he is no murderer.'

'... the blood!' implored Cecile.

'His horse, perhaps, bit him. He whips it most cruelly, you know. My brother is only happy when tormenting some creature. I live in hope that the beast may yet aim a kick at his head.'

Lucrezia tossed her hair and gave a whinny, then dissolved into laughter. 'Besides which, who do you think my brother has reason to take such vengeance upon? Be reasonable, dear one.'

Cecile forced herself to smile. Lucrezia was right. She'd leapt to conclusions and was being absurd. Nonetheless, something in the conte's demeanour had repelled her.

It was upon her lips to tell Lucrezia of how she'd entered the locked room, and what she'd seen there, but her shame hung too heavily on her shoulders. Her actions the previous night had been indefensible. Best that she forget ever having crossed its threshold.

She would speak to Lady Courcy in a few days' time, suggesting that they return to the villa—or take a trip along the coast, finding other accommodation for a while. Lucrezia, perhaps, might like to accompany them.

She'd succumbed to a dangerous enthrallment, but she would find a way to banish the madness threatening to possess her.

LUCREZIA AND CECILE dined with Agatha, consuming Magdalena's *calamaretti fritti,* in honour of the festival of Sant' Andrea, and sweet *tiramisu.*

Lorenzo was absent, taking a plate of cold meats in his room, as Lucrezia explained. Cecile was inwardly relieved.

Once Agatha had retired, Lucrezia led Cecile through to the library.

'While the tiger is away, we little rabbits shall play.' Lucrezia poured two generous measures from the decanter discreetly refilled by one of the many servants—the very same from which Cecile had helped herself the night before.

She blushed at the remembrance, then shivered, recalling the bloody fingerprints left upon Lorenzo's glass.

'Come outside, *cara,* and see the beautiful sunset. We shall welcome the twilight as we drink my brother's expensive brandy.'

Walking down through the garden, they sat on one of the middle-terraces, with a view across the water, back to Scogliera. The air tasted of orchid and oleander.

'I love this hour, so full of promise, before the dark embraces you.' Lucrezia touched her glass to Cecile's.

Taking a sip, Cecile closed her eyes. Though she didn't

enjoy the taste, there was something wonderful about the burning warmth.

'You see the lights?' Lucrezia nodded her head towards the far off shore. 'They are celebrating the festival of the *calamaro*, the squid, thanking the sea for its rich harvest. They begin by carrying the icon of Sant'Andrea to the harbour, and blessing the water, but the rest of the day is spent in feasting and merrymaking, until they can barely stand up. If the wind were to change, you would hear their music.'

'Andrew the fisherman apostle,' mused Cecile, her head already hazy from alcohol. 'Have you been to the festival many times before? I mean, wouldn't you like to be there now?'

'How thoughtful of me you are, my Cecile, but I prefer to be here with you. I have seen enough drunkeness to last a life-time. Besides which, the causeway is covered by the high tide. We couldn't go even if we wanted to. My brother asked, most particularly, that we did not go. He says that such festivities are for peasants, and that we, as noble *ladies*—' she stood to conduct a mock-curtsy, '—should hold ourselves one step removed.'

'And do you always do as he tells you?' Cecile touched the glass to her lips again, allowing herself to be a little mischievous.

'*Mia cara!*' Lucrezia gave Cecile a kiss upon the cheek. 'Come! We shall be disobedient in other ways, and he shall never know.'

She guided Cecile through the wisteria walk and down the steps, past daisies and briar roses and wild mint, their feet releasing the scent of thyme. At last, they emerged through hanging honeysuckle into the olive grove, reaching the place where they were hidden from view. The sea was close, lapping at the rocks, and there was a slight mist on the water.

'Help me. I am going to swim.' Lucrezia turned, indicating

the buttons on the back of her dress. With fingers slightly numb, Cecile did as she was bidden.

When it was loosened, Lucrezia withdrew her arms and stepped out, to stand in her shift. 'There's no one to see.'

She removed her underthings, and pushed the slip from her shoulders, until she stood bare, arms open to the breeze on her skin.

The swell and curves of Lucrezia's body were much like Cecile's own, yet different in many subtle ways. Cecile couldn't help but stare a little.

'You'll catch cold,' Cecile looked away. 'Or someone will come!'

Lucretia placed her finger to her lips. 'Just you and I.'

The tide was at its highest, not rushing up to send its spray flying, or receding with great, sucking breaths, but gentle, its sound dark and deep; a lovely, liquid undertone to the night.

I'm dreaming, thought Cecile, as she allowed Lucrezia to remove her gown. She stared at the pale glimmer of her arm. Without her clothing, she hardly felt like herself. Instead, she was a snowy owl. One shake of her wings and she might fly away.

Lucrezia slipped in, then dove beneath, emerging with wet lashes, water dripping from her nose. 'Come. Everything is wonderful.' Cupping water, she sent an arc to wet Cecile's feet.

Cecile perched on a rock, smooth against her bottom. She'd only ever bathed from shallow-sloping sands. Never in this way, slithering from rocks—and never altogether naked.

The sea glinted mackerel-silver in the moonlight. She wondered how cold it would be.

Resolving to be brave, Cecile eased herself from the rock. She exclaimed, then laughed. The water was cool and slippery, caressing every part of her. Kicking her feet and sculling, she bobbed in one place.

'Much better!' Lucrezia grinned. 'Ladies shouldn't stand

without their dresses in the evening air. We have our modesty to think of!'

They both giggled and Lucrezia reached for Cecile's hand, guiding it beneath the water.

Only a dream.

Cecile's palm was placed against Lucrezia's breast, where her heartbeat thumped strong.

Their lips were so close that it took no effort at all for them to meet and Cecile found that Lucrezia's mouth was as warm as she'd known it would be.

The waves moved over their shoulders.

'Don't be afraid, *cara*.'

Under Lucrezia's touch, Cecile melted into the water, swirling deeper. Her voice rose in small gasps and half-swollen cries as Lucrezia drew her into the closest of embraces.

'Hold on to me, *piccola*.'

A rippling, surging force was lifting her, and Lucrezia's eyes, looking into her own, were fierce and brilliant.

20

SCOGLIERA WAS STRUNG with flickering lanterns, through the trees and along the cobbled alleyways.

Masked and costumed, Maud led Henry down the hill into the village: Columbina to his Pierrot.

They ducked through the crowds, past revellers dancing in the fountain of the market square, trousers rolled up and skirts tucked into bloomers. Wearing homemade *bauta* masks for the festival of Sant' Andrea, the patron of all fishermen, they lacked the grandeur of their Venice counterparts, but their disguises did well enough, freeing them from their everyday selves. To the whirling melodies of accordions and violins, dresses slipped from shoulders, and shirts were thrown aside.

Maud was looking for something, like a beast prowling by night, the savage heart of Mademoiselle Noire beating in her chest.

There was a dark side to every coin, even when it appeared to shine brightly. Though her face was hidden, Henry could sense the tension in her body, and the strangeness of her mood.

The rising wind threatened to blow the lanterns from their ribbons. One escaped its tether and blew down towards the harbour, heading for the open sea.

As they reached the end of the main thoroughfare, the illumination grew dimmer. The bacchanal of the square seemed suddenly far away.

A group of five were sitting at a table on the street, with a flagon near emptied. There was an underlying hunger in the hunch of their shoulders, as they swilled their wine and wiped their lips.

Henry attempted to steer Maud back the way they'd come but one of the men called out and raised his glass. Harlequin in a half-mask, painted black, his eyes gleamed beneath arching brows and the bump of his devil's horn.

'*Siediti!*' He invited Maud to take a chair.

She conversed in fluent Italian, while Henry was obliged to listen, understanding barely one word in ten, but comprehending all. The men laughed at her flirtation and jokes, and all the glasses were refilled.

'These gentlemen came by carriage from Sorrento. They've asked if I might like to lie down for a while. Later, they'll drive us to the villa—and stay, if we wish for company...' She kissed his cheek.

He could only watch as she took Harlequin's hand.

AS MAUD STEPPED upon the carriage footplate, Harlequin placed his gloved hand around her ankle, and she was struck by a distant memory; another hand, grasping the same place, in the house of her great-aunt, Isabella.

She looked down at that half-masked face, and saw that it was he. The realization made her laugh. He might grasp as tightly as he dared, but she would never be his.

'I believe we've met before,' she remarked, 'Though we're yet to gain an intimate acquaintance.'

'Shall we rectify that, sweet cousin?'

She had stood upon the brink many times, knowing that a chasm lay before her yet unable to resist the precipice; no matter that some things were better dreamt of than lived, and some best avoided altogether.

She would not be captive to fear. She would not conform, nor hide. Hers was the Wild Hunt, racing outward, upward, fusing with the night.

As Harlequin buried himself beneath her skirts, she thought of the other men at the table, waiting their turn.

Rancliffe entered her thoughts only fleetingly.

This moment was not for him.

It was for her, and her blood, burning black.

MAUD'S HEAD lolled at last, sent into slumber by the powder artfully blended with her wine.

Returning to the table, Harlequin nodded to three of his companions. Only one was needed to master the reins; the other two could join her inside.

'What the deuces do they think they're doing!' Henry shouted as the horses spurred into a canter.

Harlequin and his man blocked his path, the larger of the two placing a robust hand in the centre of Henry's chest.

'Your lovely wife has found her entertainment elsewhere,' said Harlequin. 'We shall return her when she is tired of us… or when we have tired of her, *signore*.'

'The devil take you!' Henry sent a bunched fist into the man's face but failed to see the flagon raised to crack his skull.

'*Complimenti*, Serpico.' Harlequin dabbed at his nose with

his handkerchief and pushed his unconscious rival with his foot. 'You are ever to be relied upon.'

21

It was late as Cecile and Lucrezia made their way back to the castle. The library doors onto the upper terrace were no longer ajar, but one of the windows had been left on the latch.

Cecile's arm was slender enough to reach through but the sudden creaking of a hinge made her draw back.

There was a scuffle of footsteps, laboured breaths, and the heavy thud of a closing door.

'Be still,' warned Lucrezia. Around the curtain's edge, she watched Lorenzo discard mask and gloves, then put on his smoking jacket over his gaudy costume. He sank into an armchair.

Lucrezia strained to follow the exchange between the conte and his man.

'What are they saying?' whispered Cecile.

Lucrezia shook her head, unsure of how much to reveal. She wasn't party to every plan conceived by her half-brother. Nor did she wish to be. There were some wickednesses of which she would prefer to remain ignorant.

'He has someone waiting for him,' Lucrezia explained. 'He's

going to see her tomorrow. He says that she'll be ready by then.'

'I don't like being here. Can we try another door?' Cecile gave Lucrezia an imploring look

Lucrezia nodded. She had no inclination to linger. 'If we follow this wall all the way, we'll reach the courtyard by the kitchen. The door is always unlocked. Go quietly. I shall wait for you there.'

Lucrezia moved off on silent feet, and Cecile raised herself into a crouch to follow. However, a certain name caught her ear.

'*Avrò la mia vendetta contro la Signora Maud,*' snapped the Conte. '*Se lei non sarà mia moglie, lei sarà la mia puttana!*'

The way he spat the words sent ice through Cecile's veins. *Vendetta* meant revenge—but why would he wish such a thing upon Maud? As for the rest, it made no sense at all. *Moglie* was the word for wife, she was sure, and *puttana* was the sort of coarse word she shouldn't know at all—along with various others Lucrezia had taught her.

Whatever he was speaking of, his tone was unmistakably hostile. Was Maud in danger? Cecile made to beckon back Lucrezia but she was already too far away.

Cecile knew what she must do. If she stood to one side, they wouldn't be able to see her, but she might more easily hear what was said. There were bound to be a few words within her knowledge.

However, as she slid upwards, her back to the wall, her sleeve caught the protruding catch of the shutters, tearing the fabric and grazing her arm. A whimper escaped her.

'Serpico! *Chi è là?*' The words had no sooner left Lorenzo's lips than his man sprung to the curtain, drawing it back. Cecile stood in horror as the window was flung open, and she was dragged through like a scrap of rag.

Deposited crudely upon the floor, her every sense

protested at her treatment but some instinct warned her to remain meek.

The conte surveyed her calmly before addressing her not in English but with a string of Italian phrases. She comprehended that he was asking if she were hurt—and with such politeness! However, she kept her countenance without expression. He was testing her, no doubt, and she must ensure he believed her understanding rudimentary.

After some hesitation, he appeared convinced and switched to her own tongue. 'What a pleasant surprise, Lady McCaulay.' He helped her to her feet. 'Though I cannot begin to speculate as to why you're sneaking about like some secret spy. If you desire my company, you have only to enter in the civilized manner, through the door.'

Cecile had no notion of how to answer but, in any case, the conte didn't wait to hear what she might have to say. Taking hold of her arm, he steered her towards the desk. The wooden edge pressed hard behind her, and he loomed above, looking down through half-closed eyes.

'You are breathless.' He lifted a tendril of damp hair from her neck and she shivered at his touch, despite all that her mind told her.

'So predictable.' He sighed. 'Women are all the same, protesting more for show than through true humility. If I tore the gown from you, this very moment, would you avow your chastity?'

'Indeed I would!' Cecile attempted to shake off his hand. 'I was merely passing the window, having taken a short stroll on the terrace. Now, I wish to retire to my room. Your behaviour belies your breeding, and I wish no more of your company.'

With a cruel laugh, he lifted her bodily onto the desk, his hands making quick work of throwing up her skirts. With a cry of dismay, she pulled backward but only gave him greater purchase in forcing apart her legs.

'I grow tired of gallant manners. Let us call a thing by its proper name.' He bestowed upon her his predatory smile. 'Tell me that you'll marry me and I shall spare you the indignity of giving me your maidenhead upon this desk.'

'You cannot mean!' The blood rushed to her ears.

He wouldn't dare! No man would stoop so low.

'Come the morning, I shall leave—and we will forget that we were ever acquainted.' With imploring eyes, she looked to his manservant, but he stood impassive.

'How quaint you are.' The conte slid his palms a little higher. 'Serpico, as you can see, is in no hurry to come to your aid. If you squirm, I may ask him to hold you down, while we endeavour to conceive an heir. Afterwards, you shall be less coy.'

His tongue wetted his lips. 'Even your brother, I imagine, would entreat wedlock on your behalf—knowing what might be growing in your belly. I wonder if he hadn't that very plan in mind, in allowing you to reside so unprotected under my roof. The Lady Agatha is a poor chaperone against such a suitor as I.'

Cecile made to scream but Lorenzo pushed his hips hard between her thighs, and brought one hand around her neck, choking the cry within her throat. As he did so, she caught sight of the bloody bandage and was reminded again of the night before. If she refused him, would he bring violence upon her? Might he strangle her or knock her unconscious, and then have his way?

He must have seen the terror in her face, her eyes wide-staring at the crimson-seeped cloth, for his teeth revealed their wolfish smile.

'A wildcat stronger than you bit me, and she shall be sorry for it yet. Now, tell me. Shall I arrange for the padre to pay a call, and you may plan a wedding as pretty as you please, or shall we see how delightfully you submit under duress?'

Cecile fought the desire to vomit. Whatever attraction she had felt, the scales had fallen from her eyes. His countenance was devilish.

However, she made herself still. Her only hope was to play along. At first light, she would beg for Lady Courcy's help and would escape this place forever.

'There's no need for you to force yourself upon me.' She was too filled with anger to meet his gaze. 'I will concede to your wishes in the wifely manner, once we are legally wed.'

'Ah, my sweet!' Releasing her throat, he raised her fingers, laying upon them a light kiss. 'A postponement then, until our nuptials are declared. Only remember, dear Cecile, that there is no going back on a promise. Should you attempt to do so, I shall spin a tale for your brother that will do just as well as the enforcement of the deed.' His moustache twitched with suppressed mirth.

Her distress, it seemed, only amused him.

Stepping back, he allowed her to find her feet and, although Cecile's legs threatened to fail her, she brushed down her gown and took the lamp held out by the conte.

As if in a trance, her feet walked one before the other, passing through the door and mounting the stairs.

THE CONTE WENT to pour himself a restorative from the decanter.

'Lady Cecile looks fertile enough, does she not, Serpico. Once she is with child, I shall confine her to these walls. As the new contessa, I may entrust her in watching over what is most inconvenient to me.'

Feeling generous, Lorenzo, poured a small measure for his manservant. 'It will do very well, and I might visit once or twice a year, to ensure the addition of other di Cavours to the succession.'

He smiled. The more he pondered on the plan, the greater was its attractiveness. He had no desire to have his habits hindered by the presence of a wife and, once he'd enjoyed the novelty of her body, his interest would wane. Her intellect was insufficient to engage him, and her conversation too lacking in sophistication. On state occasions, perhaps, he might have her brought to him, to appear before the royal court. She would do well enough.

Lucrezia was another matter.

She, I cannot spare. Where I go, she must accompany me. Her defiant outbursts of invective are most appealing. She'll make a satisfying mistress, and her acquiescence is inconsequential. If offspring are the result, they may be raised alongside my legitimate heirs, here, at Castello di Scogliera.

'One more thing, Serpico.' Lorenzo swirled the liquid in his glass. 'Some housekeeping is in order. Our guest in the tower has been making herself increasingly meddlesome, and Vittoria is too often careless in securing the bolts. I take no pleasure in the decision, but we must change her accommodation.'

Returning to his armchair, he eased off his boots. 'Wait until all are sleeping, and secure her in the crypt. The key to the manacles you may place upon the hook at the foot of the stair, alongside those for the other doors. Bring down her bed and other comforts. I fear I cannot trust her with a candle, but you may fix a small lantern high from the ceiling, to be kept lit only during the day. Her mind, I fear, has fallen to such chaos that no recreation may alleviate its suffering. She has no solace in reading or other pastimes, so the lack of greater light may be of little consequence.'

'*Naturalmente, maestro.*' Serpico gave a stern nod.

'I've been too soft of heart, and I see it is a failing. I'd hoped to return her to some civilized version of herself, to make amends for the abuses of my father, and calm her troubled spirit. I see that my hopes were in vain. Some wounds cannot be undone, the scars running too deep. A woman's mind, as well as her body, lacks the strength of a man's. It is one of life's truths, is it not?'

Lorenzo's eyes alighted on the pair of ancestral pistols mounted above the fireplace.

As for the other matter, when my sluttish cousin reveals to her milksop my part in her abduction, her gallant knight may call me out in a duel. My aim is true enough, but I dislike uncertain outcomes. Better to settle all, with my bride's prompt signature upon the register, and oblige the English puppy to call me 'brother'.

A double revenge, to be sure— upon Maud herself and that English fop.

Pouring another large brandy, the conte found his spirits lifting. How satisfying it was to see events turned so amusingly to his advantage.

22

TEARS OF SHAME smarted in Cecile's eyes. How foolish she'd been, entertaining notions of playing the grand contessa. She'd permitted herself to be flattered, ignoring the truth of the man before her. Now, she knew him for what he was: a fiend without scruples, willing to blacken her name, poisoning her brother's ear, convincing him she was a "fallen woman". For all the modern-thinking Henry had adopted of late, would he countenance the conte's suit purely to save her honour?

And for what reason had the conte set his mind upon her for his bride?

She could make no sense of it.

Would Lucrezia be able to enlighten her? Misgiving twisted Cecile's stomach. Where had her friend been when she'd needed her?

For now, Cecile sought only the safety of her room—to close the door and sob her shock and humiliation. But, as she reached the final passageway, she saw Lucrezia waiting for her.

Raven hair stark against the white of her gown, she was trying the latch of Cecile's door.

Cecile called out but, as the woman turned, Cecile's breath froze in her chest; for the figure was not Lucrezia, though her eyes burned with the same intensity.

'Who are you?' Cecile's voice wavered.

The woman swung about. Her mouth moved, though no words emerged.

Cecile called out once again, this time pleading. 'Don't be afraid. Tell me who you are.'

The woman lifted her arms and Cecile saw that she clutched a bundle before her; a bundle from within which a delicate face was visible, surrounded by swaddling.

Dear God! Who is she? And the baby?

Cecile stepped forward, directing the lamp to shine upon the tiny form. As she did so, the woman gave a tortured wail. Staggering back, she clasped the child to her chest—far tighter than any mother should.

'Wait. Stop!' Cecile cried out, but the woman had already fled, wretched, into the darkness.

CECILE STOOD MOTIONLESS, unsure of what she'd just seen. She'd only glimpsed the child briefly but its face had been so pale, so still...

Part of her wanted to run after the poor creature; a stronger impulse urged her to retreat to the safety of her room and bolt the door.

How had she ever thought the castello a place of light and happiness. All she saw now was anguish and grief.

A sudden hand upon her shoulder made her shriek and whirl about—to find herself face to face with Lucrezia.

'*Cara*, it is I!' Lucrezia folded her in a tight embrace. 'I waited for you by the kitchen and grew worried. Where were you?'

'Oh, Lucrezia!' Cecile flung her arms around her. 'Just now, I thought you were there, at my door, but it wasn't you.' The words came tumbling out, hardly making sense.

'And who was it?' Lucrezia pulled away, placing her hands either side of Cecile's head, looking into her eyes.

'I don't know...but I was terrified! She was so sorrowful, and in her arms, she carried...' Cecile couldn't bring herself to say more.

'Hush.' Lucrezia smoothed her hair. 'Come to my chamber. We shall be safe there, side by side, and you shall tell me everything.'

Nodding silently, Cecile allowed herself to be led. Securing the door, the two climbed beneath the covers and, with sighs of despair, Cecile related all that had happened.

REGARDING she whom Cecile had found at her door, Lucrezia would need to speak again with Lorenzo. The situation could not go on as it was. For now, Cecile had accepted her explanation; the same as she'd given before.

Lucrezia had been obliged to promise she would check on the woman's wellbeing.

She had no insight to share on the matter of the wife of Cecile's brother. Had something passed between her and Lorenzo during his time in London? He'd professed no interest, but she was inclined to think there was more to the tale. If this Maud had crossed him, she pitied her indeed—for Lorenzo did not leave offenses unpunished.

'You tried to warn me but I didn't see your brother's true nature.' Cecile's voice quivered. 'I fear he intends to visit Henry, to agree terms for my hand. If Henry hesitates, I know he'll say the most terrible things, to convince him of the necessity of a wedding.'

Lying beside her, Lucrezia thought carefully. She had begun her friendship with the English girl for one reason alone: to secure her escape from the castello and a new life for herself. Above all things, that desire had guided her actions, and the intimacy of her little swim with Cecile had been the prize Lucrezia intended to dangle before her brother. Had she not done enough to win the wager?

She would argue it was so, but an acceptance of marriage would be his trumping card.

Ire rose in Lucrezia's breast. Was this to be her fate? Submission utterly to his will? She'd vowed to murder him rather than do so—and leave the Almighty to judge her.

Perhaps though, he would let her go, once he'd tasted what was forbidden. Even the greatest taboo would lose its allure, would it not, after being overcome.

But what of Cecile?

Lucrezia was not so heartless that she could leave Cecile to the machinations of her brother. 'You are certain you don't wish to marry him? The title of contessa means nothing to you?'

Cecile swallowed back a sob. 'At first, I was captivated. Your brother is unlike any man I've met before, but there's a violence in him, and I don't understand why he's intent on marrying me when he so clearly doesn't love me.'

Lucrezia felt a strange tug within her chest.

Once, long ago, she'd believed her mother loved her. She'd waited for her to return and collect her from the orphanage. Only years later had she learned the truth—that her mother had killed herself a few days after that abandonment.

So much for love.

Lorenzo intimated that he loved her, but what did that word mean? His care was not for her happiness. He wished merely to possess and control.

His intentions towards Cecile she could only guess at. She

was biddable, of course; beyond that, there was nothing in her demeanour that would appeal to his diabolic character.

Whatever passions Lorenzo had stirred in her innocent breast, they were but fragile buds of awakening desire.

The seduction Lucrezia had perpetrated herself, Cecile seemed not to associate with the 'love' between a man and woman—as if the caresses Cecile had accepted from her were the dues of friendship alone.

And what did Lucrezia feel?

An unexpected fondness and a desire to protect.

Cecile was as helpless as a kitten, and Lucrezia had a soft place in her heart for such creatures.

'Rest now.' Lucrezia stroked Cecile's cheek. 'In the morning, we shall speak with Lady Courcy. All will be well.'

Soon, Cecile fell into slumber, but Lucrezia could not quieten the fierce revolutions of her mind. One way or another, she would find release from her imprisonment, from the clutching grasp of this cursed place.

23

HENRY WOKE in the alleyway behind the bar, his face pressed to the dirt, and his jaw aching. He was alone, and a cold fear gripped his heart.

He must find her.

At the harbour, the tide had passed its highest point and was now on the turn. Meanwhile, most of the revellers had succumbed to alcohol-induced sleep, wrapped in the arms of friends and lovers. Masks lay discarded on the cobbles.

Making his way back to the villa, he located a gun and a horse, and headed back through Scogliera, taking the coast road.

The sky was a bleeding bruise of ink and purple, seeping and spreading, covering the moon and obliging him to set an agonizingly slow pace. His eyes strained to make out the edge of the cliff, and to keep his horse safely guided.

It was eerily quiet, without a single birdcall. Even the incessant rush of the waves was muffled, concealed by an ascending mist. Creeping from the sea, it rose upward to drift across the road. Were he to ride blindly, he might find himself straying to the precipice.

Dear God, may the carriage containing Maud not have fallen from this path.

The air was damp and heavy, smelling of metal, swaddling him as he plodded on. The toss of his horse's mane and its snorting breath were more tangible than his own hands, deathly white, numb upon the reins.

She might be in Sorrento by now, hidden somewhere I'll never find her, or placed on a boat. Who knows what dastardliness those curs have in mind... And here I am, barely able to see two steps in front of me.

Anger and fear tore at his chest. Maud had never allowed her actions to be curtailed. She was reckless and self-destructive, but he had known that all along. He had vowed to be her protector. If she were hurt, he would never forgive himself. If she were lost to him forever...

Whatever dread trembled beneath his skin, fluttering like a living thing, he would never give up searching.

As the first fat splashes of rain broke from above, hitting the baked dust of the road, his mare stumbled. The wind gusted and, for a moment, he thought he heard his name called, faintly, from afar. He listened again, but heard no more —only a distant rumbling of thunder—and was about to continue when something brushed his lip.

The clouds parted briefly, bringing the moon's illumination. What had blown across his face but a strand of hair, long and auburn gold. He twisted it about his finger: a thread binding her to him, and he to her.

She was not in Sorrento. She was close. With uncanny conviction, he felt it, and that her life was in danger.

Surveying the cliff rising sheer above him, he detected a break in its line. A crevasse. Wide enough for two horses. Wide enough, perhaps, for a carriage.

He nudged his horse onward, entering the passage, following until the narrow trail led to open ground, the rock-face receding. The hillside was forested beyond, pines flanking a rough track. There was no sign of habitation but, rounding a bend, two horses came into view, turned loose to graze. Behind was the carriage, its door left carelessly ajar.

His heart began to pound.

She was here.

The track had ended, the trees closing in, preventing Henry from riding further. Dismounting, he tied his mare and squinted through the dense foliage.

Not far off, there was a prick of light.

Pushing through, he made towards it, ignoring the scratch of low branches. The glow grew stronger, and he was arrested, at last, by the silhouette of a cabin. A single window was visible, one shutter rotten and hanging loose. From there, lamplight shone.

He crept forward, skirting the side to peer through.

What he saw chilled his blood.

A SHUTTER WAS BANGING.

With a start, Cecile sat upright. Where was she?

Not her chamber but Lucrezia's. Despite the noise, her friend was still asleep, her arm thrown above her head.

A hollow mistral moan enveloped the fortress walls.

Rising to secure the shutter's latch, Cecile looked out to the open sea. A mist was coming in, tendrils creeping through the olive grove and the bowers of honeysuckle below.

The terraces were scattered with fallen blooms, flowers torn from their stems, the garden's beauty blighted.

How quickly all had changed. Only short hours ago, she and Lucrezia had swum at the foot of those rocks now lashed by fierce waves, and she'd thought herself free as she never had been before.

Now, she was trapped—reliant on others to save her from what the conte intended. Though she felt weary to the bone, she knew there would be no more sleep tonight.

Wrapping a shawl about her shoulders, she sank into the armchair at the foot of the bed. Her temples ached, but her powders for such head pains were in her room—and she had no desire to venture beyond the door.

Closing her eyes, she took several deep breaths.

All will be well. I must have faith. Lucrezia will help me. Lady Courcy shall speak for me. And my brother loves me too much to force me into a marriage of convenience.

Lucrezia mumbled and the mattress creaked.

What would Lucrezia do, caught as I am, compelled against her will?

Cecile had never met anyone so outspoken. She couldn't imagine Lucrezia doing anything that didn't comply with her wishes. She was fearless, and brave.

Cecile ought to be more like her—yet here she was, too scared to fetch her headache powders; afraid, even, of the sorrowful woman who walked the corridors, though that poor creature appeared more terrified than she.

I must show more courage.

Rising, Cecile lit the lamp given to her earlier by the conte. Turning the flame low, she approached the door, but heard a scuffle of feet and a brutish voice on the other side. Not the conte's refined tones but someone else.

'Sta 'zitto! Non lottare! Donna del diavolo!'

In reply, there was an animal-whine, as of a pitiful being held in the jaws of a huntsman's trap.

Cecile froze. Her fear, trembling so near the surface, rose to choke her. Resting her forehead on the oak, she squeezed shut her eyes. Counting her breaths, she reached twenty before the sounds retreated, leaving only the battering wind beyond the shutters.

I won't hide! Not anymore!

She drew back the bolt and lifted the latch. All was still, the passageway empty. Steeling herself, she slipped out, closing the door quietly behind. She'd almost reached the balustrade of the main staircase when she paused.

What if the owner of the voice were on the landing between the two flights of steps? He might see her lantern as she passed.

She left it tucked into the wall and, ducking low, spied between the bannisters.

Through the gloom, she made out a tall figure, broad of back. He was carrying a woman in his arms, her hair hanging loose, her head lolling. Cast upwards, her face was pale in the darkness and, though her mouth was slack, she still clutched the swathed bundle to her chest.

Where was he taking her? Surely, the servants' quarters were in the upper levels of the castle—unless things were topsy-turvy here. She supposed they might be. Perhaps the servants slept below stairs, near the cellars. What did she know of the workings of an Italian household.

She might ignore what she'd seen. The woman was clearly unwell. She was being taken care of—Lucrezia had assured her. But what of the baby? Why was the mite so very quiet? It was unnatural.

That, she could not overlook.

Leaving her lantern, she felt for the edge of the steps with slippered feet, taking each with care. She would keep to the wall and trust the shadows to hide her.

As she reached the landing, moonlight from tall windows either side of the castello's great entranceway showed the man crossing the hall. She recognized his profile: the hooked nose and prominent brow. The conte's man, Serpico.

Heaving the woman in his arms, he pushed open the library door.

The library?

What reason could there be? Had the conte called a doctor to attend her?

Cecile hung back. Lucrezia had mentioned that her brother kept late hours. If Lorenzo might yet be in the library, she'd no desire to stumble into his company—and yet, she could not return upstairs without knowing more.

Creeping forward, Cecile saw that Serpico had not closed the door completely. She might glance through and ascertain who was within, and what was afoot.

As she drew closer, it was strangely quiet. With one eye, she peered within. The library was unlit, and empty but for Serpico and the woman he carried. Going directly to the right-hand side of the room, he perused the shelving, as if seeking a particular title. Then, she saw him touch one of the spines. To Cecile's surprise, the wall moved, opening a dark space.

Serpico, bearing his human burden, entered.

Though her heart was pounding, Cecile darted forward but, too late. The shelves slid back into their former position. Looking at the books ranged before her, she couldn't begin to guess which unlocked the mechanism. Her hands traced book after book, pushing randomly at those most likely, without success.

There was no hope of her following.

CECILE AWOKE to Lucrezia shaking her arm.

Her lids fluttered momentarily. The room was far too bright, the shutters and windows having been thrown wide. The night storm, then, had passed as quickly as it had come.

'Here, *cara*. *Caffè* for you.' Lucrezia pushed a pillow behind her back and the bitter-sweet aroma wafted beneath Cecile's nose. 'We have a guest, *amica*, though I cannot say a welcome one.'

'A guest?' Cecile opened one eye and almost sent the coffee flying.

The conte was seated at the foot of the bed.

'*Mio Dio!* You look at me as if I were Lucifer himself, risen from Hell! Do you smell sulphur?' He seemed rather pleased at the idea.

'*Buongiorno,* my Cecile. How is my *futura sposa* this morning? I see you have been sharing confidences, and that my sister is the first to hear our joyful announcement.'

With shaking hands, Cecile accepted the proferred cup and took a sip.

Lucrezia, wearing a robe of green silk embroidered lavishly with orchids, skirted the bed and stood by the window. Though she did not look at her brother, her comment was clearly directed at him. 'A certain member of the household has been walking in her sleep again, and has given Cecile a fright. We should supervise more closely, do you not think? We cannot have so much wandering, and rattling of doors.'

'Ah, *sorella*. Be assured, the matter is already in hand.' The conte smoothed the outer brush of his moustache. 'Although, perhaps Lady Cecile has too vivid an imagination. She has been reading her novels, I suppose, and her fancies have taken flight. Women's minds are too impressionable for such stories. In the half-light, we see what we wish to see, as well as what we fear. Sometimes, of course, the two are the same. Then again, perhaps it was the White Contessa—though the castle has many ghosts, and doors are no hindrance to them.'

At this, Lucrezia whirled about, her anger barely contained. 'Tales are not summoned from thin air. They are inspired by real events, often filled with more misery than the brain can fathom. As to novels, men only rile at us reading such stories for fear of us emulating the transgressions within their pages. I, for instance, might suddenly take a notion to be guided by my namesake, she who used her knowledge to poison her rivals, avenging deceit or insult.'

'You are right, of course. There is nothing of which we are incapable, if only we set our minds to it.' The conte fixed Lucrezia with a penetrating eye.

'Lucrezia would never commit such an atrocity,' declared Cecile, an inner force driving her to speak. 'What humanity can we claim if we lack our code of morality?'

With a sigh, Lorenzo reclined slightly upon the coverlet. 'I doubt that anything other than a sense of self-preservation prevents my sister fulfilling her little fantasy.'

Appearing entirely unperturbed, he inspected his fingernails. 'If she chooses to poison someone, no one shall suspect her but the worms, who may suffer indigestion at second-hand from her efforts. Fortunately, she knows that were any such malady to befall me, Serpico would avenge me with all alacrity.'

'If I do poison you,' sneered Lucrezia, 'It will be to save Cecile from becoming your wife.'

'The next contessa will gain not only status and wealth, but a husband able to satisfy her. What more does a woman want?' Saying this, the conte reached for Cecile's hand, raising it to his lips.

It was all she could do to avoid turning in disgust.

'Wives must take their husbands as they find them,' he mused.

'And why should a woman take a husband at all?' retorted Lucrezia.

'Women are mortal flesh, just as men. And the flesh must be clothed, and housed, and warmed through the long hours of the night. Now,' continued the conte, rising to leave. 'Cecile should speak to Magdalena about preparing a wedding feast. While the causeway is clear, I shall ride over to the villa, to tell my future brother-in-law our happy news. I shall let him know that I'm not one to insist upon a virgin bride, and that I found you to be all you should be, my dear, until the very point of acquiescence. He will, I'm sure, agree that the marriage should occur without delay. Servants do gossip and he shall wish to secure the honourable reputation of his sister.'

'*Diavolo!*' Lucrezia hissed.

'The devil is always in fashion. Though I'm told one has to have been good in order to appreciate being bad. The devil is a fallen angel after all.' The conte smiled at Cecile as he opened the door. 'I doubt that I shall join you at dinner, my love, for some other business awaits me. An old friend with whom I have an account to settle. I fear it may take some time to reach satisfaction, and I plan to drive a hard bargain.'

As soon as the conte left the room, Cecile buried her head in her hands, unable to control her tears.

'There, there,' soothed Lucrezia, immediately at her side. 'Together, we shall be stalwart, as the English say. Lady Agatha will write a letter to your brother, setting all to rights.'

She handed Cecile a handkerchief. 'If you wish it, we may make altogether new plans for your happiness. A modest income from your brother, perhaps, and I have jewellery that will fetch enough to live on for some time. We might be our own selves, and not think of marriage. Would you like to rent a small cottage in your English countryside, *cara*—where we might play music, paint and write?' Lucrezia placed her arm about Cecile.

'Could we really do such a thing? Might we?' The picture was an attractive one.

But, with that rush of hope, Cecile recalled what she had yet to tell Lucrezia—of what she'd witnessed in the dead of night. How could she procure her own freedom while a woman remained in the castello in distress? At the very least, she must attempt to discover where the poor soul and her baby had been taken.

Giving her nose a hearty blow, Cecile composed herself and told the story, throughout which Lucrezia listened intently.

'I fear something dreadful is afoot,' Cecile concluded. 'Before I make my escape from here, I must set my mind at rest. Will you look with me Lucrezia, to find this passageway, and where it leads to? Then, we may discover what has become of this woman.'

LUCREZIA DIVERTED HER GAZE, saying nothing for a moment.

She'd thought herself strong and this English lady weak, but admiration welled within her, and something akin to remorse. Her own inclination had been to flee and not look back. No doubt, her principles were ill-formed. A childhood of manipulating others to ensure her comfort had given her little compunction to act otherwise than in her own interests.

She'd long known who resided in the tower, and the story of why she was there.

'For her own good,' Lorenzo had told her. 'What life would she have? She's a danger to herself, and all around her.'

Lucrezia had allowed herself to believe that to be true. It had been convenient to do so, and she'd chosen not to bring complications on her head. Now, she felt a creeping shame.

She nodded. 'We shall look, but first we go to Lady Courcy, that she may write to your brother, and we shall make our plans.'

2 6

ANY MAN of reason has pondered that, perhaps, there is no Heaven, nor Hell, no eternal bliss nor damnation. In which case, our actions are of no significance, for good or bad, but that we must live with the memory of them.

What consequences are there for taking a life? For leaving a man with a mortal wound?

Henry had been tempted to shoot them all dead. Three bullets for three heads. There were few practical skills associated with his class but, at least, he was used to handling a gun. He knew how to take aim and gently squeeze the trigger. He could thank his father for that, though it had been years since he'd been obliged to put his marksmanship to the test.

He was not one for violence, but how should a man behave when the woman he loved was in danger. What scruples could possibly apply?

His first bullet had passed clean through a shoulder, the next shattered a knee. The third was never fired. His fury had burned no less fiercely, but he had found himself unable to injure a man who'd prostrated himself upon the floor. It had been easy enough to tie them with rope.

He dared not think what Maud had endured in those hours before he'd found her. Placed before him on his horse, his cloak wrapped tight around her bruised and bloodied body, her back leaning into his chest, she was barely conscious, subdued by her injuries and the potency of her sedative.

The return journey was perilous, the steep track turned to mud by rain. His mare lost its footing more than once, sliding its descent with rolling, panicked eyes. The obscuring mist sat thick along the coast road. He hugged the cliffs, plodding at a steady pace and avoiding the worst of the torrent by keeping close. To do otherwise would be treacherous. And all the while, his hand lay upon Maud's heart, comforted by its abiding beat.

Reaching the villa, he slid her from the saddle and carried her in, to the warmth of their bed. She roused a little at the removal of her wet clothes, her arms rising to defend herself, yet too weak to open her eyes.

'There, my love, you're safe now,' he whispered. 'I'm here, and I shall be always.'

THE HOURS PASSED, Henry fearing to leave her side. Despite the fire's warmth, she shivered. Waxen-pale, a fever consumed her. Her pulse had fallen to barely a flicker, and her breaths came shallow. Her lips were paper-dry.

Patiently, he wetted them, before passing the dampened sponge about her neck.

'Be careful when you love something wild,' she'd once said. 'You may wake one day and find that it has flown, or crept or scampered away, leaving a space which cannot be filled by anything tame.'

Maud, don't leave me. You can't leave.

He'd spent his life looking for her. How could he bear to lose her, now that she was found?

Taking her limp fingers, he kissed each one. Slowly, so slowly. He paused before reaching the smallest, pressing her palm to his cheek, wanting to hold the moment. He laid his head upon her chest, seeking to hear her heart, but she was so still, as if already departed. He spoke her name, but she didn't answer.

His tears came then, a distillation of his rage and sorrow until, face wet with all he could not say, he fell asleep, Maud's chill fingers still clasped in his.

MAUD DREAMT.

First, she was climbing a ladder. Something, or someone, was pursuing her. She needed to reach the top, without knowing where the ladder led.

Next, she was on the mortuary slab, dissected, her organs removed, one by one, before being laid in the cold earth, in a hole where the worms waited.

When she woke, it was to a sensation of heaviness on her chest. She tried to push it away but her fingers found soft curls and the shell of Rancliffe's ear, his jaw rough-stubbled.

She was thirsty and her body ached, but there was a feeling of strength too. She'd touched the veil separating us from the next world, and had lingered long in that dark place. She'd tossed between life and death, but she hadn't surrendered.

WHEN THE CONTE DI CAVOUR arrived to seek a meeting with Rancliffe, he found the gentleman to be indisposed.

'What a pity,' Lorenzo remarked to the maid who took his card. 'No matter. Give his Lordship my felicitations on his marriage. I have some acquaintance with his charming wife, and am now delighted to enjoy the same with his sister. I'll return another day. Perhaps I may join his Lord and Ladyship in taking afternoon tea. Such a civilized custom.'

The conte could barely contain his merriment as he mounted his stallion.

No doubt, he sits in his room and wrings his hands for his abducted darling. Fear not, for she is in my firm custody, and I ride to visit her now. I shall give her every attention, and ensure she remembers the day she spurned the advances of a di Cavour, in favour of the milksop love of an English lord.

'GOOD MORNING, my dear. Now, I've no intention to slight where your heart has chosen'— Lady Courcy motioned to the seat beside her in the morning room, while offering her cheek for Cecile to kiss—'but I cannot hold my tongue. My nephew tells me you've accepted his proposal of marriage, and that we should expect a new contessa before the week is out.'

She paused, as if searching for the right words. 'My dear, it's all most sudden! Am I to believe that a proper courtship has taken place? That he has won your heart? That you are convinced of his suitability as a husband?'

Cecile found that she must sit, for her legs would no longer support her.

'Of course, the conte is undeniably handsome and a man of status, and no inconsiderable means...' Cecile looked at Lucrezia for help but her friend made no contribution other than nodding her encouragement. Cecile needed to speak for herself.

'If you're sure that this is the path to your happiness, I'll be the first to congratulate you.' Lady Courcy frowned a little.

'But I wish you to assure me that you've given the matter proper consideration. To act in haste is folly, as the marriages of so many demonstrate.' Agatha gave a heavy sigh. 'It's true that wives choose, often, to be blind to the indiscretions of their husbands, but is this what you wish for yourself, Cecile? For I cannot believe that the tiger will be turned from its nature.'

Cecile felt, suddenly, quite sick. Lady Courcy truly believed she intended to accept the conte's suit. Worse still, just a few short days ago, she'd begun to entertain the idea herself.

Agatha picked at a dainty meringue, crumbling it onto her plate before looking sharply at Cecile. 'I understand he intends to acquire a special license. I must say this hurriedness is unseemly. People will talk, Cecile.'

Her face was not that of an excited bride, Agatha couldn't help but notice. In fact, Cecile looked decidedly wan. Agatha lowered her voice, speaking with more gentleness. 'Forgive my indelicacy, my dear, but I must ask. Is there reason for this celerity? Have you permitted the conte... freedoms? You are young, I know, and the passions of a whirlwind courtship can lead us astray. You would not be the first young woman to find herself in a difficult situation.'

'Lady Courcy,' Cecile took a deep breath. 'The conte's ardour has been difficult to keep at bay—but I have not succumbed to any action obliging marriage, no matter what the conte may infer. I fear he has made up his mind without any consultation as to my own feelings.'

'I see that I am right. You are not ready to be married.' With a little cough, Agatha dabbed her napkin to her mouth. 'You wish to delay?'

'I do.' Cecile raised her chin. 'In fact, I wish to avoid the marriage altogether, but I'm fearful of what the conte may say to my brother to persuade him of the necessity for a hurried ceremony.'

She couldn't look Agatha in the eye. 'I know the conte to be a proud man. He shall be offended if I protest too strongly. Better for him to realize in his own time that we are not the match he wishes to believe.'

'Of course, my dear. Say nothing more.' Agatha folded her hands in her lap. 'I shall write this moment to Henry, explaining all, and shall speak to Lorenzo on his return. If he values your hand, he should be prepared to wait for it. It's indecent for him to bully you into marriage, and improper to fail to observe a courtship of adequate duration. He is too used to having his own way.'

Cecile's eyes showed her gratitude.

'Like all men!' scoffed Lucrezia. 'They think only of their own desire, assuming reciprocity, and that everything can be accomplished in the twitch of a tail. Cecile shall not be manoeuvered into marriage.'

'Marvellous, Lucrezia. Your tenacity does you credit.' Agatha rose, placing her hand upon Cecile's shoulder. 'What it is to have good friends. One day, as a married woman, you'll find them just as important as you do now. More, perhaps...'

With that, Agatha swept from the room. 'I shall show you my letter for the earl when we meet for luncheon, my dears, and we may send Raphael to deliver it this afternoon.'

LUCREZIA KNEW ALREADY which book must slide back to engage the mechanism. Her fingers found it easily, and the gloom of the stone passageway was revealed to them. A cool draught rose from the opening, and the smell of damp stone.

'Where does it lead?' Cecile peered downward.

'You know the place. Where the di Cavours lie in their tombs. There's more than one door to that chamber,' explained Lucrezia.

As they descended, the dark was palpable. Cecile's hand traced the rough granite of the wall, using it to feel her way. The lamp, held aloft by Lucrezia, threw little enough light, making it difficult to see the edge of the steps. Cecile feared she might stumble but, at last, they reached the lower level.

Water was dripping. Small bodies scuffled and scuttled.

'*Ratti*,' said Lucrezia. 'Let's move.'

Their breathing was so loud that it seemed to fill the space, but Cecile was sure she heard another's breath in that subterranean cavern; inhaling, exhaling.

Lucrezia raised their lamp higher, illuminating the tombs down either wall. It was cold, there, in that buried place. The skin on Cecile's back prickled, as if something unearthly touched her from the shadows, something wild and terrible. She felt eyes upon her, beyond the meager pool of light in which they stood. Eyes which had watched long, seeking her out, wishing to communicate.

The flame of their lamp sputtered, eaten by the darkness, and a mournful wail began to rise, curling from the walls in an unravelling ribbon of grief and pain, as if the stones of Castello di Cavour bemoaned the long hours of silence, and their own centuries of suffering.

Lucrezia clutched at Cecile's arm. '*Così terribile!*'

'We'll do this together.' Cecile didn't feel brave, but she knew she must convince herself to be so.

The wail subsided, replaced by a scraping sound, as of nails against stone.

'Can you hear it?' asked Cecile.

The sound came again. A scratching, ahead of them, deeper in the crypt. As they moved forward, there was the smell of decay, of old meat, of sour flesh. And a faint glow.

At the far end of the chamber, a figure crouched upon a bed, hair long and tangled, her face turned away. Her nails dragged across the stone, lifting periodically to renew the motion, hands cuffed and chained. When the woman raised her head, her eyes were sunken and her face deathly.

'*Mio Dio!*' exclaimed Lucrezia. 'Livia!'

The woman jerked at the utterance of her name.

Cecile's instinct was to draw back, but this was no monster, and there was no malevolence. She was flesh and blood and her nails, though blackened and broken, were those of no demon, but a human wretch.

'It's alright,' Cecile whispered, whether to herself, or Lucrezia, or this poor creature. 'It's alright.'

Cecile took the final steps towards the woman, bending to take her hands in her own, refusing to be deterred by the unwashed smell of her body.

The woman's mouth moved, as if to speak, her voice rasping, but the sounds she wished to make were unable to leave her tongue. They remained half-formed, dying in a stutter.

'These are like the manacles Lorenzo placed about my wrists that day.' The remembrance of it, of her own quickened pulse, of the strange excitement it had roused in her, now made Cecile feel nauseous. For who could be responsible for this but the conte. Nothing happened in the castello without his direction.

'There are keys, near the staircase. Wait here, Cecile, and I shall fetch them. One may open these cuffs.'

Before Cecile had a chance to answer, Lucrezia had moved away, taking their lamp with her. Despite the dim lantern suspended overhead, the darkness seemed to flood into Cecile's eyes, her nostrils, her ears. All the horrors of that place whirled within the rushing dark. Her consciousness swayed inside her.

To be left here alone, without sufficient light or warmth, without anyone to care. What mind would not be disturbed by such imprisonment, such isolation?

Livia's fingers pressed hers tightly.

When Lucrezia returned with the lamp, Cecile's own face turned towards its welcome light.

It was the work of moments to fit the key into the lock and release the bolt, revealing the skin of Livia's wrists, rubbed red.

'Come with us,' Cecile urged.

'Cecile,' warned Lucrezia. 'We cannot!'

Cecile stood, attempting to raise Livia to her feet, but she cowered away, reaching for the bundle beside her on the bed.

'Come with us,' said Cecile again. 'We can't leave you here.'

But the woman who was once Livia had closed her ears, twisting her face to the wall. As she pulled the bundle towards her, Cecile saw again the tiny face, with its open, upturned lips.

Not a baby, but a doll.

'YOU TOLD ME SHE'D DIED,' admonished Cecile as they retraced their steps to the light. 'But you knew all along; knew she was here—somewhere in the castello.'

'I didn't tell you all of the truth. What good would it have done for you to know everything?'

'I might have married him,' countered Cecile, 'Not knowing what he'd done!'

Passing through the library, Lucrezia hurried Cecile outside. 'I will tell you all I know. But not here. In the garden.'

How long ago it seemed, that first day, when Cecile had explored the fragrant terraces, and delighted in the cascading of lush blooms.

Once upon the lower terrace, Lucrezia looked behind them, as if to check they were unheard and unfollowed. 'I told you most of the story. You remember that Livia had a baby? It was Camillo who visited her in the night, her own father. It's no wonder that she lost her wits. Lorenzo tells me he remembers hearing her crying, but she would never speak of it.'

'But, her mother, Isabella—surely she knew!' The thought of it made Cecile sway. Her mouth tasted of bile.

'Perhaps not. They say that mothers do not always, or that they cannot allow themselves to believe.' Lucrezia shrugged, but her own face was pale.

Cecile looked out at the sea, upon which the sun sparkled brightly.

It seems so cruel that we feel the warmth and light, while one who might sit with us, had life treated her more kindly, remains in darkness.

'They hid her away, in the asylum, not just for the wild behaviour she began to exhibit, but to conceal the pregnancy. The baby died, but she did not, and whatever remaining sanity she possessed ebbed away. Through grief I suppose, and being put in such a place. I'm sure we'd lose our reason too, under those circumstances.'

'It's too barbarous.' Cecile grimaced.

'When Lorenzo first brought me here, he showed me her tower. Her room was simply furnished but she had a window, and one of the servants would sit with her. I believe that, when he claimed her from the asylum, he hoped to offer her a life of some comfort. He was brave in some respects, for his own mother thought Livia to be dead. Lorenzo could have lived with the same lie. Instead, he found her, and returned her to her family home.'

Cecile couldn't help but frown. 'And now? She's too inconvenient, so is parted from all humanity, confined in that dreadful place. This I can't forgive him.'

'I agree that we cannot leave her there,' conceded Lucrezia. 'But I don't know what we may do. The strings of the mind, like those of a violin or piano, easily run out of order, and I fear Livia can never be mended.'

Lucrezia took Cecile's hands in hers. 'I'll speak with Magdalena. There's a passageway from the crypt which runs under the sand, to Scogliera. A relative of Magdalena may agree to look after Livia. Money can always be found. Lorenzo is generous in the purse he allows the kitchen. We might say that she fled and drowned, if we leave her clothes upon the rocks.'

'Yes; perhaps.' Cecile wiped a tear from her eye.

'But then we too must disappear. We aren't safe here. Despite these plans to bide time, my brother will not be content. I fear his spite will turn on us.'

The sun was warm, yet Cecile couldn't help but shiver.

'*Mia bella.*' Lucrezia placed her arm about Cecile's shoulders. 'This place is too full of others' history, reaching into the present. We should make our own history now.'

'*IMBECILLI! SCIOCCHI! LI MALEDICA!*'

Muttering more curses, Lorenzo tore at a cobweb brushing his neck and returned the lantern to its hook, with a brusqueness that caused the glass on one side to crack.

So many plans carefully laid, conceived over months. And to have them foiled by a mere foppish aristocrat! It was intolerable!

Despite her rescue, Maud would forever remember her experience as an unpleasant one. However, Lorenzo's desire for revenge over his imperious cousin had been long-awaited, and he'd been denied the climax of his entertainment. He was accustomed to gaining satisfaction, in all things.

Damn those peasant imbeciles I engaged to guard her and damn this tunnel!

Both hands were needed to open the door which led from the passageway beneath the sands into the dank crypt of the castello. The tides had fallen particularly inconveniently of late, covering the causeway just at the hours when he needed to move on and off the island. Privacy, like all things, came at a price, but his bones were not growing any younger. The subterranean damp discomforted him.

The door was stuck again, the wood expanding in its frame with the flow of water above. Serpico, walking behind his master, was obliged to put his shoulder to the oak to heave it open.

'I shall block this passage and have done with it. Better to return to my Siena residence and leave this place altogether. Coming here after so many years travelling has been a mistake,' grumbled the conte. 'Only the contents of the library and my private collection of curios have given me amusement, besides the occasional girl from the village—and such women are to be found anywhere. Serpico, you must arrange transportation. Have them sent on. My artworks too, of course.'

'Sì, maestro.' His manservant pushed the tunnel entrance closed once more.

The figure in the corner cowered as they passed, but they didn't look her way.

LORENZO HAD BEEN DRINKING for many hours, having begun before dinner: a solemn affair, in which neither his bride-to-be nor Lucrezia were willing to return his conversation.

Hell take them!

Lorenzo was tired of waiting. In the morning, the padre would come, early, as soon as the tide receded and his horse crossed the sands.

They'd speak their vows in the chapel, without guests, or wedding gown, or flowers. He'd drag her from her bed if necessary and hold her upon her knees before the altar, but he'd have his way.

She's of the age of consent. Once we're joined in the eyes of God, no one shall have the power to challenge our union. She'll do as she's bidden, and her brother may gnash his teeth all he likes, without authority to interfere.

Lorenzo raised the decanter once more, but it was empty.

How long had he been plagued by this hopeless longing? He'd yearned for something, but known not what, wasting time and energy in pursuit of endless distractions. Now, he knew what he wanted. An heir! She'd bear him fine children, he was certain, and they'd be his legacy. Sons!

The seas were eternal, as was the wind, and thunder and all elementals, but not human flesh. It withered and faded. The body was finite. Even the brightest light might be extinguished, and he was weary to the bone.

Was it the curse of the White Contessa, bringing down her ill-wished prophecies on the men of his line, or was it his own wickedness that led him on devilish paths? His heart was a night garden of buried deeds, in which virtue had been strangled by venomous creepers, poisoned by the serpent's fang.

His head was growing heavy, nodding to rest on his chest. His cigar dropped from his fingers to the floor.

Quietly, the shelving in the wall slid open. Someone was standing silently, watching, having emerged from the darkness.

Lorenzo dozed, and dreamt that the crushing hand of mortality was at his throat. He wondered, as he had on other nights, who or what might await him when he crossed from this world to the next.

It was Livia who gripped his neck, her eyes alight as she squeezed her brother's last breaths from his chest.

The cigar was smouldering a dark patch on the rug. Picking it up, she held its glow to the papers on the desk. How beautifully they flared, curling to ash. Such a little thing, but look what it could do. She brushed it against a newspaper folded on the table, to a book lying open, and to the curtains.

Flames licked upwards.

A room full of paper made a feast for crimson tongues. Hot and hungrily, they consumed. The flames were undiscerning. All volumes were to their taste.

The leering devils carved into the shelves danced more merrily in the heat. Swooping down the chimney, the wind blew encouragement on the blaze.

Livia threw the cigar onto Lorenzo's lap and ran from the room, her bare feet taking her up the stairs, along the corridor and to her tower room. It looked larger without her bed. She took a cushion from the armchair and hunched behind.

Best to hide, she thought. *Hide where no one will find me.*

A FIST WAS BEATING upon Cecile's door.

'Quickly!' Lucrezia implored, her eyes red-rimmed from the smoke. 'We'll take the servants' stair, down to the kitchen.'

Lady Courcy stood beside, holding an oil lamp, looking frailer than usual. Her face grey with fear, she coughed at the drifting fumes. Holding her between them, Cecile and Lucrezia had almost reached the end of the passage when they heard a long and melancholy keening.

'It's the wind,' said Lucrezia.

But Cecile knew better. 'Not the wind; it's her!'

A sorrowful, spiralling note drifted down the corridor, from the direction of the tower.

'We must leave,' insisted Lucrezia.

But Cecile was already turning back the way they'd come. 'Take Lady Courcy to safety. I'll find Livia.'

Lucrezia called Cecile's name, but she'd already gone, feeling her way through the dark, her fingers keeping contact with the wall, following the wailing lament until she reached the door to the tower.

It was open.

Lifting the hem of her nightdress, she groped upward. The air cleared as she went higher, the smoke being yet to reach this part of the castle.

The room appeared empty, but for a chair that had seen better days, its rose-brocade faded, threads loose and puckered. Tattered braiding trailed from dusty curtains, hanging forlornly from their crooked rail. A simple chandelier, empty of candles, moved in the draught, its few glass beads tinkling faintly.

Apart from this, the room was silent.

The moon shone weakly through the window. There was a mirror on the wall, mottled with age, and Cecile saw herself in its dingy reflection. For a moment, it was as if she were the occupant of this pitiful room; she the one who must be saved.

Then, behind her, something moved. The mirror showed a crouching figure. A ghost from the past, with a face bone-white and eyes beetle-dark; she whimpered.

'It's me. You're safe,' coaxed Cecile.

I'll never be safe, thought Livia.

She almost knocked Cecile to the floor as she rushed past, taking the stairs again. Not down but up.

'Livia!' Cecile set off after her.

Lorenzo's warning had some truth, for the steps were worn. Twice, Cecile slipped, grazing her shin. Smoke was rising, the smell acrid.

At last, having navigated the curving spiral, Cecile reached the upper door leading to the roof. Cast open, the brisk night air swept in. Torn strips of cloud streamed across the moon and the wind whisked Livia's long hair. Already, she was climbing onto the battlements.

'Wait!' Cecile raced to her, placing her own foot on the stone's edge.

Below, glass shattered and flames leapt from windows. Fumes belched from the fiery belly of the library.

Livia hugged the doll to her chest; the baby who might have been.

Nightdresses billowing, they looked down at the tumbling froth, at the straining sinew of the sea. Cecile reached for Livia's hand, and their fingers touched.

A rasping voice called from behind. 'Quickly! You must come!'

Cecile turned to see Lucrezia stumble out, then heard her scream.

From the corner of her eye, Cecile caught the flutter of white fabric.

Livia di Cavour had flown free.

THE WHITE CONTESSA watched over the two young women as they fled through smoke and blazing cinders. As they passed through crack and spit and roar, she blew back the flames and fumes that would scorch and choke them. In their wake, the fire leapt once more, fuelled by molten anger.

She watched the demise of the ancestral home of the di Cavours, who made each other what they were, and are.

Cecile and Lucrezia emerged at last, faces blackened with soot, to where Lady Courcy and the loyal servants of the household stood, beneath overhanging oleanders, faces raised in awe and fear, lit by the fierce heat.

And the castle remembered, as it burned.

29

MAUD SHIFTED BENEATH THE SHEETS, stirred and sighed. Her eyes met his for a long, sorrowful moment, and her lips attempted to form words. She was a scorched moth, drawn to the deadly flame. Fragile. Mortal. The soft beauty of her body its downfall.

'My darling,' he whispered. 'There's only you and me. Nothing bad. Nothing to harm you.'

What fearsome alignment of the stars there must have been —for so close he'd come to losing her.

Henry had long dreamed of unravelling the mysteries of the universe, as if they were a puzzle to solve. To this end, he'd studied the classics of Greek and Roman literature, attended dissections of the human body, and wandered the streets of London, seeking to understand human nature through the observation of each face. He believed that time would bring ultimate wisdom.

Certain forces drove us through this life: hunger, the need for comfort and shelter, and curiosity for learning. But one drove more forcefully than all the rest: our desire for love, for our heart's meeting with a kindred spirit.

He'd chosen an unbiddable wife who was a mystery to him in many ways. She was like the sea, the depths of which were inscrutable, but for small clues floating occasionally to the surface.

Now, he realized some mysteries were only ever partially understood. They were not to be solved, only to be experienced, and the greatest mystery of all was our ability to love another more than our own self.

30

'OH! *SCAPPA!*' Lucrezia was startled by a plump and hairy caterpillar investigating the crook of her elbow. 'What a vile thing!'

Reaching across the cloth spread upon the lawn, Maud
took the creature and placed it upon a nearby leaf. 'From the
unpromising caterpillar comes the butterfly. It retreats
temporarily into its cocoon and transforms, born to the
freedom of the air.'

Cecile looked up. She'd been in one of her reveries,
plucking the petals from a daisy. She threw the torn thing
away and looked at Maud. 'Can one ever marry and be free do
you think?'

'History tends to show us otherwise,' Maud replied with a
half-smile. 'But, it's up to us to write new rules. Perhaps it can
be done...'

'Of course, there's no need for you to wed yourselves to
men and the predictability that entails,' asserted Lady Courcy,
lifting the teapot. 'I am deeply sorry, my dear Lucrezia, for
your loss, and I cannot begin to imagine how Isabella will take
the news of her son's death. I shall travel to London, I think, to

spend some time with her. She will be distraught. Though Lorenzo's behaviour was not always as she would have wished, the bonds of blood cannot be denied. The loss of a child is inevitably painful.'

She visited each cup. 'I shall not presume to probe your heart Cecile, but I hope that any wound may soon be mended. The conte, I fear, would never have made you happy.'

Cecile, her eyes upon the rose pattern of her teacup, found that her feelings were strangely untouched, and the realization shamed her.

'If you do decide to marry, one day,' Lady Courcy continued, 'There will be other suitors. Meanwhile, you may be whatever you choose and, my darlings, you'll always have a home here, at the Villa Scogliera.'

'Thank you, Lady Courcy.' Lucrezia gave their hostess the warmest of smiles. 'I may be in need of your hospitality.'

Cecile leaned over to give the old lady a kiss upon the cheek.

'I shall write to Isabella,' said Maud, 'Offering my condolences. She was very good to me, during my stay with her in London.'

'She thinks of you with fondness, my dear,' said Lady Courcy. 'There was a daughter, but she died. A frail girl, I heard. No doubt, Isabella found great comfort in your company.'

Cecile and Lucrezia said nothing.

'Such a terrible tragedy.' Maud took a sip of tea. 'For that ancient castle to be razed to nothing. I visited several times as a child. The gardens are beautiful, I recall.'

'I remember taking you.' Lady Courcy looked back towards the ruins. 'Lorenzo was away at university, and then travelling —or residing in Siena, I believe.'

'Did you not meet in London?' enquired Lucrezia, 'Not so long ago...?'

Maud's eyes flashed, but she composed herself. The question went unanswered. 'Sad, also, to lose one's home. I understand that there's little provision for you, Lucrezia, in your brother's will, and some distant cousin inherits the title.'

'We were only half-siblings,' admitted Lucrezia, 'However, my jewels were in my pockets when we fled. My brother was generous in his gifts. The gems are real; as far as I know.'

'My condolences for your loss,' added Maud, almost as an afterthought, her expression somewhat distracted. 'I hear Lorenzo was apt to smoke cigars, and he seems to have fallen asleep while doing so. I'm pleased that the servants escaped unharmed.'

'Yes,' commented Lady Courcy, 'All but his man, who is unaccounted for. Serpico was seen entering the library, to rescue his master, despite the heat of the flames. Terribly brave. It speaks for some worthiness in one's character, to inspire such loyalty. Sadly, neither body has been recovered. The ceiling has collapsed and the room is quite destroyed. Better to leave them resting in peace.'

'Peace was something my brother struggled to find in life. Perhaps he may do so now...' Lucrezia hesitated, as if to say more, then looked away.

'Cecile was so brave,' added Lady Courcy. 'Turning back to save one of the staff she thought was still in the upper part of the castle.'

Lucrezia shook her head slightly, as her eyes met Cecile's.

'It was more foolish than brave.' Cecile gave a sigh. 'The cry for help I thought I heard was only the wind, whistling down an open staircase. An illusion. Nothing more.'

Lady Courcy took Cecile's hand. 'Courageous and modest!'

'Padre Giovanni Gargiullo, from Pietrocina, is coming to say prayers at the site.' Lady Courcy looked wistful. 'I'll do what I can for the staff. Raphael is to work here now, and I'll employ Magdalena. I'll write references, that all may seek employment in Sorrento.'

She gave a sniff. 'They might find it suits them better, in the end. A modern hotel offers more opportunities than a private home. Times are changing, after all.'

WHEN MAUD TURNED HER HEAD, Rancliffe was there.

'It's starting to feel like autumn, my love, with this chill in the air and leaves chasing each other about the garden. Perhaps it's time for us to leave.' He wrapped her shawl about her shoulders. 'Walk with me.'

He nodded at the others before leading her away, through the olive trees, where the breeze shimmered the slim, silver-green leaves.

'I wish to discuss something alone with you. There's an expedition heading to Brazil, organized by the Ornithological Union and the Natural History Museum. I've been invited to join them.' He turn to face her. 'I'd thought to decline, as the expedition will require us to relinquish many of our comforts, but I think the trip is just what's needed. A fresh page, putting aside all that's happened here. I must telegraph soon.'

He paused, endeavouring to read her expression. 'Don't think that I make this suggestion lightly, Maud. It's my duty to ensure your happiness, and I believe the adventure will revive you, offering opportunities for your own study. You might present a series of papers on your return, or find a publisher for your work. Your illustrations are more than fine enough. The work of the Royal Entomology Society would be enriched by your efforts.'

She sighed, before allowing herself a tentative smile. 'We can, I suppose, live as many lives as we like...' She touched his cheek.

Driven by curiosity, and by grief, she'd sought to punish and lose herself. She could not live without folly and danger it seemed, but perhaps there were other ways to court them. Some winds kept us awake, while others lulled us to sleep, and some blew out the old, leaving room for fresh approaches.

'How pleasant it is to bask in your adoration, husband.' She led them towards the clifftop steps. 'To know that you seek my own happiness in equal portion to your own.'

Her tone was suddenly playful.'I think you'd love me even if I ate nothing but garlic and cabbage.'

'Probably.' He crinkled his nose in an expression of distaste.

'And will you still when my skin wrinkles like an over-ripe apple, and my teeth come loose?'

'Even more then, for my skin and teeth will be the same— and we'll have grown old together.'

Maud paused, smiling with pleasure at Rancliffe's answers. 'And what if I spoke only of the latest fashions in hats and shoes?'

'I would, although I might have to stop your lips more often with my kisses.'

She raised her face to his, and they stood for some moments, his arms wrapped closely about her, his embrace both tender and passionate.

It was she who broke away. 'And will you continue to worship me if I grow fat, so that I waddle more than glide?'

He laughed. 'I might urge you to eat less cake, my darling, but I'll love you no matter how you're embellished.'

'And what if my belly swells not from cake, but from your love?'

He looked at her directly. Was she in earnest? He saw in her face a strange excitement. 'My darling!' Falling at once to his knees, he pressed his cheek to her stomach.

For so long, Maud had been unsure of what she sought or

how to find it. She'd been scared, of herself, and of the changes coming.

Was this how love should be? The world could be fearsome, but no more so than the unfathomable space inside.

Maud had thought some places too far for her wings to reach, but it was only a matter of flying to where she wished to go, towards the points of light in the dark.

She was still mistress of herself. She always would be.

She held her face to the sun, and felt its warmth not just on her skin but inside too. Henry's lips joined hers once more and so light and joyous were their kisses that they floated upwards, drifting through the air, swooping through the Cyprus trees.

Out, out, out they went, to the open sea.

EPILOGUE

WHOM AMONG US would not be tempted by the wild luxuri-
ance of barely discovered lands? By the vast, lush jungle? A
place of violence and beauty, in its endless, devouring cycle,
and home to untold species, waiting to be looked upon by
human eyes: joyous parrots and gaudy toucans and others
perhaps yet without names.

The night before their departure, Cecile dreamt of the
sinister night howl of monkeys. She couldn't content herself
with a quiet life. Not for her a tranquil existence in a
provincial English town, or days of ease at the Villa Scogliera.
The world awaited her.

And she wouldn't be alone.

How kind her brother had been, and Maud too. Henry was
to pay not only for her passage on the *SS Leviathan*, taking
them across the Atlantic, but for Lucrezia's too. A young
woman must have company, and she couldn't bear to be parted
from Lucrezia. They would make a jolly party.

It was without regret that Cecile stood on the deck of the
great steamer, looking down at the bustling harbour. Among

the many heads below, Cecile spotted one whose golden curls rose above those of his fellow passengers, as he made his way towards the wooden plank bridge.

Her eyesight would need to be better than it was for her to read that his luggage bore the initials L.R. Nevertheless, when he raised his face to look upon the vessel destined to take him across the high seas, Cecile had no difficulty in recognizing those bold features.

And she smiled.

What next for Cecile, Lucrezia, Maud and Henry?
Discover all, in the concluding volume of the trilogy.
Read on…
in Forbidden Seduction (also published as 'Murder on the SS Leviathan')

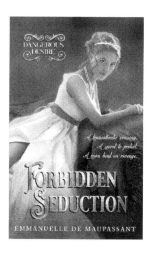

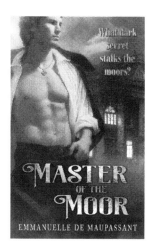

Master of the Moor

A dark mystery, a terrible secret, and a woman who is not what she seems

After more than twenty years in exile, Mallon de Wolfe—formidable, handsome, and with a shard of ice where his heart should be—returns to his ancestral home, upon the windswept heathlands of Dartmoor.

To a place vast, barren and perilous.

A place of superstition, where no man walks without the moon to guide him.

Only when the mysterious Countess Rosseline arrives at Wulverton Hall does Mallon find true reason to face the horrors of his past. Too late does he discover that the newly-widowed Countess hides secrets of her own.

Haunted by scandal, she'll stop at nothing to gain what she needs, even if it means resorting to deceit and entrapment.

'Master of the Moor' is a deeply emotional, dark gothic historical romance, featuring passionate love scenes.

The Viking Warriors Series

Surrender to irresistible seduction: a world of burning desire and brutal passion, threatened by ambition, jealousy and revenge.

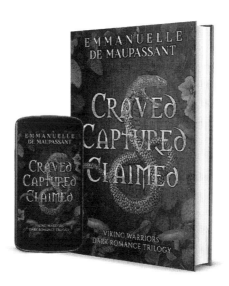

Three hardened warriors, proven in battle. But, are they worthy of a woman's love?

Burning desire and brutal passion; jealousy and revenge, betrayal, secrets and redemption. Discover what it means to be loved by a Viking.

A woman enslaved.

A battle of passion and loss in a dark and dangerous world.

Three rivals seek to possess Elswyth.

To take her liberty.

To make her their pawn.

Caught in a storm of jealousy and passion, her life hangs in the balance.

Just as she believes herself safe, an unseen enemy drags her to the depths of desire.

Elswyth must fight if she wants to survive.

Before she loses herself completely.

A pulse-pounding dark romance you won't be able to put down.

Unexpected twists that will leave you breathless.

ABOUT THE AUTHOR

Emmanuelle de Maupassant lives with her husband (maker of tea and fruit cake) and has a penchant for hairy pudding terriers (connoisseurs of squeaky toys and bacon treats).

www.emmanuelledemaupassant.com

ABOUT THE EDITOR

Adrea is a Melbourne-based freelance writer, editor and former stage director. She holds a BA (Hons) in theatre studies. Through her fiction and non-fiction writing, she engages with themes of the feminine, often focusing her lens on the rich diversity of feminine sexuality. She is also deeply interested in myth and fairy tale re-tellings. After many years interpreting play-texts as a theatre director, Adrea is now applying those skills in deepening the "theatre on the page", enhancing the writer's voice through developmental editing.

Adrea's erotic short stories and poetry appear in various anthologies, including *The Big Book of Submission 2* (2017), *For the Men (2016)*, *Coming Together: In Verse* (2015) and *Licked* (House of Erotica 2015), *The Mammoth Book of Best New Erotica 13*, and *A Storytelling of Ravens* (Little Raven 2014).

Her provocative flash fiction and short stories feature on many online sites. In another guise, she has published a feminist creative essay in *Etchings* literary journal (2013), and her short memoir story was published in an Australian anthology the same year. Adrea is working on a collection of themed erotic short stories *Watching You Watching Me* and her first novella, a mythical re-telling.

To discover more, visit her at:
https://koredesires.wordpress.com/about/

Printed in Great Britain
by Amazon

16766930R00109